CW0084131

HOLLOW POINT

HOLLOW POINT

THE SILENCER SERIES BOOK 7

MIKE RYAN

WWW.MIKERYANBOOKS.COM

Copyright © 2019 by Mike Ryan

All rights reserved.

No part of this book may be reproduced in any form or by any electronic or mechanical means, including information storage and retrieval systems, without written permission from the author, except for the use of brief quotations in a book review.

1

—————

Recker had just arrived at the favorite meeting spot of his and Vincent's. Though he was a few minutes early, he looked over at the door and saw the burly man at his usual spot, indicating his host for the meeting was already waiting inside. Recker got out of his car and walked over to the front entrance, opening his coat to remove his gun. The guard put his hand up to stop him.

"Boss says you can keep your guns from now on," the man said.

"Oh?"

"Guess he figured since you saved his life you get a free pass now."

"Well I suppose I'm entitled to some benefits from it," Recker said.

Recker walked through the door and was immediately greeted by Malloy. Though a mutual respect had

I

grown between the two men over the years, they still weren't on handshake terms upon seeing each other. It was the same as always. They gave each other a slight nod, then moved on to their business. Recker went down to the usual table, sitting across from Vincent, who had just finished his breakfast.

"Mike, how are you?" Vincent asked.

"Fine."

Vincent pointed to his plate. "Can I offer you something?"

"No, I'm good."

"Had a feeling you would be. I know you usually don't join me in these little excursions, so I took the liberty of eating beforehand."

"My eating habits have changed a little bit lately. Eat more healthy, home cooked stuff."

"A wise decision on your part," Vincent said, patting his stomach. "I think I may have put on a few extra pounds from all these outside meals I've had."

The two men shared a laugh at his self-depreciation, though Recker was still in the dark as to what the meeting was about. When Malloy called him to request it, he didn't give any indications as to the topic they'd be discussing. And Recker couldn't figure out on his own what Vincent may have wanted. It'd been three months since Recker and Haley took out the assassin who was gunning for the crime boss. Since that violent day, they'd kept their distance from each other, though not necessarily on purpose. They just had no other business that required their cooperation in that time.

As far as Recker knew, nothing major had happened recently that would cause either of them to need assistance on anything, so he was at a loss as to what he was really doing there. And Vincent wasn't one to always get straight to the point. Sometimes he liked to run in circles for a little while until he reached his destination. Something Recker would just as soon avoid.

"So what's this about?" Recker said, hoping to speed things up a bit.

Vincent smiled, always appreciating how his guest liked to skip the formalities and get down to business. "Always the straight shooter."

Recker shrugged. "I dunno, I just figure we're both busy people, have a lot on our plate, why prolong things? Plus, we're on good terms, no need to beat around the bush, right?"

"Indeed," Vincent said, wiping his mouth with a napkin. "I just thought we might chat about a few things that have happened over the last several months. Some things that I've been hearing."

"Such as?" Recker asked, not having the slightest idea about what he was inferring.

"Well, I've been hearing that business has picked up quite a bit on your end."

"It's been pretty steady. That's really nothing new."

"No, but you must be tired. You seem to be spreading yourself pretty thin lately."

Recker shook his head, knowing there was something else Vincent was leading up to. "I'm holding up just fine."

"I'm sure. You have broad shoulders, a passion for this line of work that never dies or wanes."

Recker grinned and scratched the back of his head, still waiting for the purpose of the meeting. He wasn't yet irritated by the runaround, but was growing a little impatient. He tossed his left hand in the air to indicate he didn't have any response.

"Very well, I'll stop this little charade that we're having," Vincent said, picking up on Recker's clue that he wasn't partaking in the game anymore.

"I'd appreciate it."

"There's been some rumors, some rumblings, that you've expanded your operation lately."

"There has?"

Vincent nodded. "It's been brought to my attention that there have been witnesses to you working with another man. Word seems to be getting around."

Recker looked stone-faced, as he knew Vincent usually picked up on visual clues to his questions as much as he listened to the actual responses. And this was a question he really had no interest in answering.

"You know you should never believe everything you hear," Recker said.

"A very good business practice."

"So, is that it? That's what this is about? The possibility of me having more assistants out there?"

Vincent nodded, and looked at the ceiling, measuring his words carefully. "We have a good relationship that we've built up over the years. Whether you have other people you're working with or not isn't really of my concern. You'll do your business in whatever way you see fit."

"Then what's the issue?"

"Well, as you know, a man in my position has to be well aware of what's going on around him. Has to know all the possible players in the field, who's on the same side, who are enemies, what might be some possible situations that could have to be dealt with at some later date in the future."

"Whether these so-called rumors are true or not isn't really something you need to be concerned with," Recker said, still not giving in.

"Well, that might be something that we disagree on," Vincent replied, motioning with his hands for emphasis before folding them together on the table.

"You should know that whether I do or do not have help out in the field isn't something you need to worry about. It has nothing to do with our arrangement."

Vincent nodded, knowing he was unlikely to pry out of his visitor the information he was seeking, though he still felt the need to ask the questions. "So, if these rumors turned out to be true..."

"Then, presumably, it might be something as

simple as just having someone out there to watch my back. Hypothetically speaking," Recker said, sticking to his guns and not revealing what they both knew to be true.

It wasn't necessarily that he was trying to hide the information from Vincent. Recker always knew he'd probably be among the first to find out, especially with his contacts all over the city. It was more of a personal thing with Recker. He just didn't want to admit to anyone there was a new member of their operation before it was necessary. For Vincent's part, he wasn't going to continue to force the issue. He felt he had the answer to his question, whether Recker admitted it or not.

"I can see how, hypothetically, something like that might be a good idea," Vincent said. "Especially with some of the situations you wind up getting placed in."

"Yeah."

"I hope you don't mind the probing questions. I'm sure you understand my position, always having to be aware of any new players in town."

"No, I get it. But as far as you and I are concerned, nothing changes."

"Good to know. So how has David been these past few months?"

"Good. Busy."

"I can imagine. An operation such as yours must take a lot of time to maintain."

Recker shrugged. "We make do."

"I guess if you ever did take on another partner, it'd enable you to spend more time at home with your girlfriend."

Recker's eyes almost bulged out of his head hearing him talk about his girlfriend. It wasn't something he'd ever mentioned in any of their conversations. He hoped Vincent wasn't about to strong-arm him the way Jeremiah tried to, putting Mia in the middle of things. Vincent could see his guest looked a little unnerved with his statement and tried to put his mind at ease.

"Relax," Vincent said, putting his hand out. "I'm not trying to dig into your personal life, or create some type of friction or anything. I've already heard how that turns out."

Recker lifted his head up, not saying a word. But he didn't have to. His facial expressions did all the talking for him.

"Yes, I've heard about how Jeremiah tried to use her to get to me."

"How?" Recker asked.

"You forget, there are still a few of Jeremiah's men roaming around," Vincent said. "I've been able to have the pleasure of speaking with a few of them."

"And what'd they have to say?"

"Just how they tried to use the girl to persuade you to do their dirty work. Obviously, that was an epic fail on their part."

"It would be an epic fail on anyone's part," Recker

said, trying to give a warning without making a direct threat. Nobody would ever use Mia to get to him again.

"I would agree. She was the, uh, the nurse that I helped to rescue, wasn't she?" Vincent asked with a smile.

Recker shuffled around in his seat, just about ready to light into his host with a bunch of words he probably shouldn't say. He somehow could put those thoughts aside for the moment and remain diplomatic.

"And just what do you plan to do with all this newfound knowledge of yours?"

"Nothing," Vincent answered. "We're just two friends sitting here, discussing our lives like regular people do."

"Except we're not regular people."

"True. But I think it only serves to strengthen the bond between us. There are rumors that there is another dangerous person in town, perhaps working with you, perhaps not. But I'm not worrying about it because you have told me there's nothing to worry about."

"Yeah?" Recker said, knowing he wasn't done with his speech.

"And I know you have a girlfriend who works at a hospital. A woman who has been caught up in a dangerous game before by a man who was obviously losing his grip. And it's not something you should worry about because I'm telling you there's nothing to worry about."

"I think I see where you're going with this."

"We've been through a lot together these past few years, haven't we?" Vincent asked, almost happily recalling memories most normal people would rather forget.

"Yeah, I guess we have. So, how's it felt being the only main player in town these past few months?"

"Well, there's always going to be minor nuisances here and there. People who want a bigger piece of the pie. Nothing that's really at a threatening level though."

"And are you satisfied with that? The power and territory that you have now. Or is there still more you'd like to accomplish?"

"Well, as you know, my enemies disappearing these past couple of years has happened at a surprising and breakneck speed. There's still much to do just maintaining and growing the business of what I now have. I'm quite comfortable with that for now."

The two men continued talking for another twenty minutes or so, neither saying anything of much significance. It was mostly just small talk, passing the time. As they both got ready to leave, though, Vincent dropped another little bomb in Recker's direction.

"Before we go, there was one more small thing I wanted to talk to you about," Vincent said.

"Which is?"

"As you know, I have several members of the police department at my disposal."

"Yeah?" Recker asked, not sure where this dialog was going.

"How would you feel about meeting one of them?"

"I've already had the pleasure. If you recall, that was one of the conditions of Jeremiah's demise."

Vincent feigned a look of ignorance. "Yes, of course. This would be someone different, though. Someone who is very interested in meeting you."

"I can't say I share the same viewpoint," Recker said, not sounding the slightest bit interested in the proposal.

"I'll pass it along."

"Just out of curiosity, who would this officer be?"

"A detective."

"And just why does he want to meet me?"

"He's a fan of your work," Vincent said.

"Excuse me if I'm not all warm and fuzzy about being someone's idol, but I don't think I mix particularly well with those on the other side of the line."

"Understood, but he's not looking to arrest you. I believe he has some business he's interested in discussing with you."

"So why can't you just tell me what it is?"

Vincent shrugged. "Because I don't know all the particulars. I believe it's a police matter."

"And he didn't share with you?"

"Well, just because he's on my payroll doesn't mean he isn't his own person. I don't get firsthand knowledge of everything that comes across his desk."

"Just the things that pertain to you?" Recker asked.

"Or things that I have a personal interest or stake in."

"I'm not sure that meeting with a detective is something I'm really interested in doing right now. I don't think it's too wise for me to play around too frequently with people who have the ability to lock me up."

"As you wish. I'll deliver the news if that's your final answer. I'm sure he could make it worth your while, though."

"No, it's OK. I still think I'll pass on the offer. The more I associate with the police, the surer I'd be that something would eventually go wrong."

"Always play things cautiously," Vincent said.

"No different than you, right?"

Vincent nodded. The two men only talked for a few minutes more before Recker excused himself and left the diner. He called Jones as soon as he left to let him know there wasn't anything that needed to be worked imminently. As he sat there in his truck, he looked over at the diner again, thinking about some of the things that were said. It was a strange request, he thought, Vincent asking him to meet with a police officer. Recker wasn't sure what to make of it. There was obviously a reason for it. And it was probably a big one. But whatever it was, if it was as big as he imagined it was, he assumed he'd be hearing from Vincent again on the subject.

When Recker got back to the office, Jones and

Haley were sitting side by side, analyzing some information they'd been working on. Recker poured himself a cup of coffee and walked over to the window, not wanting to say anything to the pair and throw their concentration off.

"Are you just going to ignore us, Michael?" Jones asked.

Recker turned around to face them. "Looked like you were deep in thought there. Didn't want to disturb you two lovebirds."

Haley chuckled as he kept his eyes glued to the screen. Jones, though, pushed his chair away from the desk to further engage his friend. Recker's eyes danced around the room, like he was thinking about something. It was one of the clues Jones had picked up on in the time they'd been together. It usually was an indication something was bugging Recker. And usually, it wasn't a minor thing.

"So, what is it?" Jones asked.

"What's what?"

"You know. That thing you're thinking about."

"What makes you think I'm thinking about something?" Recker asked.

"Do we really have to play this game? Whenever you have a problem or something on your mind that you're not ready to discuss, you have that look on your face."

"What look?"

"The look you have right now," Jones said. "The

one where you have trouble focusing on any one thing in particular. You look out the window, glance at the floor, sometimes the wall, perhaps the ceiling, or maybe a few other inanimate objects."

"Do you analyze me often, doctor?"

"Just when the situation calls for it."

"Oh. Very scholarly of you, professor."

"So, would you rather just get it out now or do you wanna have a song and dance for a couple of hours first?" Jones asked.

"Oh, I dunno. Who's gonna lead?" Recker said, continuing with the joke. "I mean, I forgot to bring my dancing shoes with me today."

While Jones didn't look very amused, Haley couldn't help but laugh again, overhearing their conversation, though he was still typing away on the computer.

"So, I take it you're insisting on the 'let's talk for a while until I pry it out of you' method?" Jones asked.

Recker tried to keep a straight face and continue with the charade, but just couldn't hold it in anymore and let out a laugh as well. Jones took a step back and took turns looking at his two Silencers and simply shook his head.

"I was hoping your sense of humor wouldn't emulate his," Jones said, looking at Haley.

Haley didn't reply. He just smiled and went back to what he was doing. Recker seemed to be enjoying the back-and-forth tug he and Jones were having. But, he figured enough was enough and finally came clean with what was on his mind.

"If you must know, I was thinking about Vincent," Recker said.

Jones scrunched his eyebrows together, wondering why the crime boss would be deep in his friend's thought process. "Why would you be thinking about him? You said nothing of much interest was said at the meeting. Was there more?"

Recker shrugged as his eyes shot past Jones, looking at different parts of the room. "Well, I dunno."

"What do you mean, you don't know? Either something was said, or it wasn't."

"Right before leaving, Vincent asked if I wanted to meet with a detective that was on his payroll."

Jones looked perplexed by the request. "For what purpose?"

"He wouldn't tell me."

"Seems a bit odd."

"I know. I can't figure out what it could have been about."

"Was it any of the ones that you met outside Jeremiah's house on that final day?"

Recker shook his head. "No. Said it was someone else. But, Vincent said it wasn't of his asking."

"What do you mean?"

"Vincent said this guy, this detective, asked to meet with me. Had nothing to do with Vincent. He was just acting as the intermediary."

"Well that is strange indeed."

"You don't think Vincent could be setting you up for something, do you?" Haley asked, finally interjecting himself into the conversation.

"No. I think we're still on as good a terms as we've always been," Recker replied.

"I wonder what it could be about?" Jones said.

"I dunno. I'm sure we'll find out soon enough, though."

"Were there any other interesting nuggets from the meeting you'd care to disclose?"

Recker shrugged. "Uh, he said he's heard rumors of another person being with me, so he asked if we had a new man in the operation."

"Oh?"

"I didn't confirm or deny anything."

"Well if you don't deny something, it's as much of a confirmation as actually confirming it," Jones said.

"Yeah, but I did it in a much more amusing way."

"Oh, well, as long as you had fun with it," Jones said, rolling his eyes.

"He knows we've got another man whether I actually admit it or not. The only thing he's really worried about is knowing who it is."

"Why?" Haley asked.

"You don't get to his level without knowing every person in the city who's capable of posing a threat to him at some point," Recker answered. "He just wants to make sure you're not someone he has to worry about in the future."

"So, will he?"

"No, I basically told him how it is. He's not gonna concern himself with it too much now."

"How can you be so sure?" Jones asked. "If you recall, he poked around quite a bit, asked several questions to try to get to the bottom of our operation initially. Unless of course you forget about Mia and I ducking out on Malloy down at the university."

"I haven't forgotten."

"Then how do you know he won't try to find out Chris' identity?"

"Because we came to an understanding," Recker said.

"An understanding? Care to expand on that?"

"He took me at my word that our new man has nothing to do with him and is nothing he needs to be concerned with."

"He did? Seems very unlike him to just accept something like that so easily."

"Well, it also might have something to do with me taking him at his word about something."

"Which is?"

"He knows about Mia," Recker said.

Jones just stared at him for a few moments. "You'll have to divulge a little more. He's always known about Mia."

"He knows she's my girlfriend."

As soon as he said the words, Jones stood there, stunned. Haley, too, stopped what he was doing and looked at Recker. It was a startling revelation for them.

"Seeing as how you don't seem too terribly upset, I take it you're satisfied with whatever it was that Vincent told you," Jones said.

"Well, he said he's heard about why that little beef with me and Jeremiah happened, with Mia being used as bait. And he knows where she's working."

"Well we've always suspected that."

"Yeah, but that's why he's not worried about Haley. He doesn't need to worry about our secret and I don't need to worry about his."

"So, he's basically letting you know he knows about Mia, but he'll never do anything to her, unless he's provoked," Haley said.

"That's basically the size of it."

"Is there anything else you'd like to share about this meeting?" Jones said in a huff.

"No, that was it."

"That was it. You initially told me nothing interesting happened, and yet, you just disclosed three different topics that were extremely noteworthy. Are you sure there's nothing else you'd like to share?"

"No, that's it."

"It seems as though we have different definitions of what's important."

Recker shrugged again, not giving it much more thought.

"Even if the other things can be shrugged off, I do wonder what that business with the police is about," Jones said.

"Well, if there's one thing I'm sure about when it comes to dealing with Vincent..."

"What?"

"We'll find out soon enough."

2

W ithout having a specific case to work on right then, Recker and Haley had gone out to lunch. Jones stayed behind to work on a few leads. He hoped to have a new case later that night or the following morning. They brought back a sandwich for their leader, who immediately started devouring it, holding it in one hand as he continued typing with his free hand.

"Take a break, David," Recker said. "It'll still be there in a few minutes."

Jones looked at his friend and nodded, pushing his chair away from the desk momentarily. "Did you two enjoy your lunch date?"

"Very nice. Food was great," Haley said.

"Hey, how's your apartment working out for you?" Recker asked.

"Oh, I love it. It looks so good. Mia did an unbelievable job with it. She really has a nice style and good taste. She could be an interior decorator or something if she ever decided to leave nursing."

"She likes helping people too much to do that. Maybe a side gig or something."

"Well, tell her I can't thank her enough for making the place look so good. I never would've been able to do that."

Recker laughed. "She knows. That's why she did it. Probably didn't want it to look like an empty warehouse for a few years like mine did."

"Yeah, there are some days I wake up and I look around and don't even wanna leave the apartment."

"Hopefully that is only a fleeting thought," Jones said.

Mia had fixed up Haley's apartment the previous week after offering her services several times. She, Recker, and Haley had become good friends in the time since the new Silencer had arrived on the scene. The three of them sometimes had dinner together at one of their places at least once a week. Knowing how Recker treated his apartment before Mia moved in, she didn't want Haley's place to have that same devoid-of-life feeling to it. Even though they weren't in their apartments for most of the day, Mia thought they should still have a nice environment to come home and relax in. She figured it was good for their mental state to have pleasant surroundings at home, rather than blank walls to stare at.

After quickly eating his sandwich, Jones got back to work. Recker and Haley milled around the office for a little while, not having anything specific to do. Recker finally went to his gun cabinet and started cleaning some of his weapons, Haley giving him a hand.

"When's the next assignment coming?" Recker asked.

"Should be here shortly," Jones replied.

"What's the beef?"

"Possible murder."

"Oh good. Love those," Recker said sarcastically.

Recker instinctively looked over at Jones for a second, then went back to cleaning his guns. But something tugged at him that something was wrong. Jones had a concerned look on his face and seemed to be typing a little faster. He took turns working between two computers.

"Something up?" Recker asked.

Jones briefly looked at him before going back to his work. "A problem. Definitely a problem."

"Thought you said it wouldn't be ready until later?"

"No, not with that case. That's still on the same schedule."

"Then what is it?"

"A problem."

Recker looked at Haley and sighed. "Is this how I sound sometimes? Like, not giving direct answers."

Haley shrugged, not really wanting to admit it was true. They finished cleaning the guns and closed the cabinet, then walked over to the desk and sat next to Jones, waiting for him to tell them what the problem was.

"Would you like to expand on that now?" Recker asked. "You tell me I'm not very forthcoming sometimes, but you're not exactly Mr. Talkative yourself, you know."

Jones turned his head and looked at the pair and raised his eyebrows, not sure he agreed with the suggestion.

Seeing as how nothing else was working, Recker looked away and sighed in frustration. "Maybe we can help."

"Yeah, let us go out and work our magic," Haley said. "We got nothing else going on right now."

"I'm afraid this is nothing you two can work magic with. At least not yet," Jones replied.

"Jones, just spit it out. What's going on?" Recker finally asked, tired of the games.

"Well, it appears there was a shooting sometime this morning. I'm still trying to figure out the particulars."

"So, how's that pertain to us?"

"Yeah, unless they missed. If they didn't, should already be a police matter, shouldn't it?" Haley said.

Jones gave him a serious-looking face. "It is indeed a police matter. It seems as though the target was one of their own."

Recker took a few seconds to let what he said sink

in. "What do you mean, one of their own? You mean somebody shot a cop?"

"That is exactly what I mean."

As Jones continued typing, Recker and Haley looked at each other, both understanding the seriousness of the situation. It was something none of them liked to hear. Recker put his hand over his mouth as he looked at the floor. His mind thought back to the situation involving Officer Perez and Adrian Bernal, causing Recker to make a deal with Vincent to find the would-be killer. After a few seconds, Recker broke free of his trance.

"Is the officer dead?"

The look Jones gave him told him all he needed, though Jones clarified it anyway. "Unfortunately, yes."

"What happened?" Haley asked.

"I'm still trying to piece things together."

"How'd you pick up on it?" Recker said.

"Only because the police have called a press conference for thirty minutes from now," Jones replied.

"So why didn't we pick up on it?"

"You know the reasons as much as I do. There's no crystal ball to pick up on these things. We can only pick up on what's planned... and shared. If it's not premeditated, or texted or called or emailed to an accomplice, you know we won't get wind of it. Not beforehand, anyway."

Recker sighed, already knowing as much, still frustrated nonetheless. "I know."

"If it's someone who just decided this morning to do something like that, then what can we do?" Jones asked.

"Nothing," Recker said, shaking his head.

"Believe me, Michael, I know it's unfortunate, and it bothers me as well, but sometimes we can't be there in advance."

"Especially with police officers," Haley said. "They get involved in so much stuff, a lot of it is just spur of the moment. Could've just been a routine call that escalated somehow."

Recker nodded, everything both men were saying making sense. It didn't make him feel better, though. Jones continued typing away, fiddling in his seat the way he often did when he found something that piqued his interest. When that happened, he tended to sit straighter as he looked at the screen. Recker noticed he was doing it now.

"You got something else?"

Jones gulped before answering, not liking what he was seeing. "It appears that there was another shooting of a police officer three days ago."

"What?" Recker incredulously asked.

"Three days ago, another police officer was shot. He was a little luckier, though, in that he survived."

"Did you already know about this?"

"It's the first I'm hearing about it."

"Why didn't we know about this already?"

"It wasn't publicly known until now."

"What?" Recker asked again, not believing it. "Since when has the shooting of a cop not been publicly known? That's usually a lead news story in any media outlet."

"I don't know, Mike, all I can tell you is what I'm seeing."

"There's gotta be more to it."

The three men didn't say another word for fifteen minutes, as Jones continued digging into the shootings. He finally found the reason they didn't hear of the first shooting.

"It appears that the police department kept the first shooting hush-hush," Jones said.

"Why would they do that?" Haley asked.

"It seems the first officer shot was actually on an undercover assignment."

"Which means they didn't want word leaking out that it was a cop," Recker said, understanding now why it was covered up.

"Makes sense," Haley said.

"Yeah, but how are you finding this out now?" Recker asked.

"In the wake of this latest shooting, that officer was pulled off that assignment this morning," Jones replied.

"Things are getting hot."

"So it would seem."

Jones continued sifting through the information at his disposal as Recker and Haley quietly and patiently waited nearby for any further bits of knowledge he could drop down on them.

"Well that's interesting," Jones said, his eyes glued to the screen.

"What's that?" Recker asked.

"It would appear that both officers were hit with the same kind of bullet."

"So? Doesn't necessarily mean there's a connection."

"Perhaps not. But it is interesting nonetheless."

"What kind of bullet?"

"Preliminary reports indicate both were fired from a .45 automatic. Both were hollow point bullets."

Recker leaned back in his chair, thinking about what might have been going on.

"Is that too much of a coincidence?" Jones said, saying what they all were thinking.

"Two shootings in three days against the same profession with the same type of bullet?" Recker said. "I guess anything's possible."

"One officer was undercover and another in uniform. Very well could be a coincidence."

"Like I said. I guess anything is possible."

"Should we start on it?" Haley asked.

Jones shook his head as he turned to face him. "The police have already started their own investigation on it. And believe me, with two of their own being shot, they will be completely thorough."

"David's right. As much as this crap bothers me, I

don't think we need to roll on this one. They'll pull out all the stops on it," Recker said. "They'll find the guy, assuming it's just one. Even if it isn't, they'll find them."

Haley nodded, and even though he wanted to get in on it, understood the reasoning to stay away.

"Besides, we have another case to work on coming up," Jones said.

"Might be a good idea to keep an eye on the police investigation, though, just to see how it's going," Recker said.

"I will do that."

Jones went back to typing at his computer, as Recker rubbed both sides of his temple with his hand. Haley, though, wasn't ready to put the shootings to rest, thinking there may be something else involved.

"Hey, I just thought of something," Haley said. "Do you think that detective that Vincent was talking about might have something to do with this?"

Recker and Jones looked at each other, though neither said a word at first glance as they thought of the possibilities.

"Maybe the guy wanted to see if we'd heard anything about who it might have been," Haley continued.

"That's kind of a tall leap, wouldn't you say?" Jones asked. "Linking one to the other."

"Maybe. But that would classify as pulling out all the stops, wouldn't it?"

"A police detective asking help from us on a police

investigation involving the shooting of one of their own wouldn't just be pulling out all the stops. It would be destroying all the stops."

Jones looked at Recker to see if he agreed with his assessment and mentioned something to him. But considering his friend totally ignored his comment, he assumed Recker was so deep in thought he just didn't hear him. Jones let him be for a moment until his lapse of concentration had gone then repeated his statement.

"Huh?" Recker said, though he did hear his friend talking. "Oh, well, I don't know. Like I've said twice already, I guess anything's possible. I guess it would depend on their leads, or lack of them, and how desperate they are."

"I couldn't see any scenario in which they asked for assistance from us."

They debated the pros and cons of such a scenario for a few minutes until Jones pulled up the press conference on one of the computers. The three men stayed glued in their seats as they watched the event unfold, none of them saying a word throughout the proceedings. Once it was over, Jones clicked off the website and switched the screen to something else.

"Well? What do you think?" Jones asked.

"Didn't really say anything we didn't already know," Recker said. "I think it's still too soon to know what's going on even for them."

With nothing more they could really say other than they'd keep monitoring the situation, the trio got back to working on their own business. After three solid hours of putting their nose to the grindstone, their concentration was finally broken by the sound of Recker's phone ringing. As it was after five, Recker thought maybe it was his better half calling. He got up to answer it, walking over to the counter where he'd left it the last time he'd gotten a drink.

"Probably Mia checking about dinner," Recker said.

He was surprised when he picked it up and looked at the screen, seeing it wasn't Mia. It was Vincent. Highly unusual, he thought, especially after just meeting with him that morning. He also thought it strange it wasn't Malloy calling. Usually Vincent's right-hand man made the initial contact when a meeting was arranged, or they started preliminary work on a problem. Vincent usually only called if it was something urgent that needed immediate attention. Recker picked up his phone and looked at his two partners and shook his head, letting them know it wasn't Mia.

"Surprised to hear from you again so soon," Recker said.

"Well, in situations like these, urgency is required."

"Just what situations like these are you talking about?"

"I suppose you've heard about the two police shootings by now?"

"Yeah, I watched the press conference they had earlier."

"Then by now I'm sure you know the severity that the department is dealing with right now."

"Yeah. I may be wrong, but I never figured you for someone who bled blue."

"We've known each other for a few years now, Mike, you know I'm a level-headed guy. I don't believe in chaos and letting the inmates run the asylum. Police are very much a necessity in our society today. Without them, who knows what kind of nonsense we'd be running into on the street every day."

"You don't want to return to the Wild West?" Recker asked.

"Ah, it was a glorified period of violence. Anyway, back to our topic, if you recall this morning, my police contact wanted to have a word with you."

"I don't think my answer has really changed since then. Still not all that interested."

"Well, I told him of your reluctance to meet."

"So, what's the issue?"

"He has asked me if I could try again to persuade you," Vincent said.

"Why all the interest on your part? You work for him or does he work for you?"

Vincent let out a small laugh. "You should know by now, Mike, that I don't work for anybody."

"You're just doing this guy a favor by talking to me?"

"I think there's a slight misconception when people think I have officers of the law on my payroll. I don't have them out there doing illegal things, killing guys, muscling people around, dealing drugs, things like that. They're good, hardworking officers. They just get paid to distribute certain information to me."

"Or bust up rival criminal enterprises," Recker said. "Or stand by and arrest lookouts of a city center gang while a third party goes inside a restaurant and eliminates the competition? Or surround a house that has a rival leader on the premises."

Vincent laughed again. "I guess you could look at it that way."

"What exactly does this guy want?"

"I believe it has something to do with the two police shootings. He knows you're someone I've done business with, I told him you have a way of finding out things that slip through the cracks, he asked me if I could reach out to you. It's as simple as that."

"You'll forgive me for my hesitancy, but it's not every day that a police officer asks to meet with me."

"You think I might be setting you up for something?"

"It's not so much that I don't trust you, I think we've always forged an understanding between us. But as much as I respect the boys in blue, that same trust doesn't go over the line for them."

"Mike, believe me, I didn't take the risk of rescuing

you from the back seat of a police car, just to set you up a few months later. You have my word on that."

"Trust doesn't come that easily for me. I've gotten this far on my ability to read situations correctly, and being careful enough to avoid things that look a little shady," Recker said.

"And you have good instincts. But I'll tell you this, I guarantee this is not any type of setup. Not by me, not by them."

"I believe that it's not you. But what makes you think this guy's not looking for a promotion, trying to lure me out somewhere and get the drop on me? Or maybe even a guy who's got stars in his eyes and figures he can lay this whole mess at my feet."

"No, it wouldn't happen, and I'll tell you why. Because he came to me and asked me to set something up with you in good faith. Nobody uses me as an excuse to lay the hammer down. A man's only as good as his word. I know you feel the same way. How do I know it's not a trap? One simple reason, he knows I would not put up with it. If he uses my connections for a setup and makes a liar out of me, he knows, like everyone else, that after it was over, he'd be taking a swim in the river. And he wouldn't be coming back up for air."

The insinuation was clear for Recker. And though he believed every word Vincent had told him, he still wasn't sure about it. Though Recker always appreci-ated the work of the police, crossing lines, and interacting with them wasn't something he was fond of doing. Today's friendly cop could be tomorrow's enemy trying to lock him up. Still, there was something tugging at him that he should accept the meeting and find out what the detective wanted. Eventually, Recker relented.

"Fine. I'll meet with him."

"Great."

"But I'll do it on my terms. I'll name the place and time."

"Where and when?" Vincent asked.

"There's a little bar in the northeast on Grant called Gino's, you know it?"

"I do."

"I'll meet him there tonight at ten. I'll wait five minutes after. If he's not there by then, I won't be either."

"Understood. I'll convey your terms to him."

"Good. I hope they're acceptable because I won't alter them," Recker said.

"I'm sure they'll be fine. This might be a good time for your rumored friend to make an appearance."

"Well, if the rumor turned out to be true, I'm sure he would be. But he wouldn't be anywhere anyone would be able to see him."

Vincent chuckled to himself, admiring Recker's attention to detail. "I do wish you'd eventually come around and accept a position with me. We could do a lot of things together."

"Tempting offer, but I think I'll stick with the gig I got now for a while."

"I know. I've given up on possibly tempting you to the dark side for some time now. Anyway, how would you like to find out who the contact is? Want a secret handshake or something? Maybe one of you wears a certain color tie?" Vincent asked, joking. "Maybe one of you sits against the wall drinking a glass of milk through a straw?"

"That would be quite the sight, wouldn't it?"

"I would almost pay money to see it."

"I don't think we need to do anything that extravagant," Recker said. "Just tell me his name. I'll take it from there."

"Ah yes, you have your ways of finding things out, don't you? His name is Detective Tony Andrews. Been on the force about twenty years, black hair, has a wife, two kids."

"What district's he work out of?"

"Twenty-second. He's a good man, you have nothing to worry about with him. Some guys have shifty eyes, you know the ones I'm talking about. You can almost see the wheels spinning inside their heads, wondering how they're gonna try to pull one over on you. But not this guy. He's solid. You'll do good business with him. I'm sure of it."

"I guess we'll see."

Recker and Vincent exchanged a few more pleasantries, then hung up. Recker put his phone back on the counter and put his right hand on his hip, his left elbow leaning across the counter as he stood silently in thought. Though nobody else had said a word since the conversation ended, Recker could almost feel the tense stares of his two partners, beating down on him. He stood straight and looked over at them, a neutral expression on his face. Jones was the first to start hammering him with questions.

"Was that what it sounded like?" Jones asked.

"I dunno. What'd it sound like?"

"It sounded as if you agreed to make an appointment with the good detective that we were speaking of earlier."

"Well, I guess you heard correctly then."

"Weren't we talking about how it was not a good idea to do that?"

Recker looked at him strangely. "I don't recall any of us saying that."

"Oh. We didn't?" Jones asked, looking at Haley, who shook his head. "Hmm. Perhaps I was just thinking it in my head and didn't let the words pass my lips."

"I don't know, I look at it like this. We thought it was strange that an officer wanted to meet, we wondered what he wanted, now we'll know."

"Assuming it's not some type of trap set up to get you."

"You don't think it's a trick, do you?" Haley said.

"No, I don't think so," Recker answered.

"Why not?"

"Because I don't think that Vincent would allow it. It's like he told me, he didn't rescue me from a police car a few months ago, just to set me up, or let someone else set me up a few months later. It wouldn't make any sense."

"I somewhat hate to agree with the man, but that is a valid point," Jones said.

"You want me to tag along?" Haley asked.

"You know it," Recker said. "I may be trusting. But I'm not that trusting."

"Did you get a name of the guy?"

"Yeah. Vincent said his name is Tony Andrews, works out of the twenty-second."

"I'll pull his information up and see what we can find."

As Jones swiveled his chair around to work on the computer, trying to find out what he could about Detective Andrews, Recker and Haley began discussing the specifics of their upcoming late-night outing.

"What are you thinking?" Haley asked.

"Might be better to have you on the outside some-where," Recker replied. "That way you can give me a little warning if you spot any trouble."

"How about if I sit in a car outside? If something comes up, you duck out the back and I'll fly around to the back door and speed out of there."

"Probably the best option. Either that, or you set up across the street with a rifle."

"Yeah, but if I do that, and trouble pops up, I might not be able to get to you in time. You might get surrounded."

Jones couldn't help but hear parts of the conversation and wanted to put his two cents in. "I think Chris' idea is better."

"Probably," Recker said.

"But neither strategy accounts for the possibility that the police could surround the building before he's able to get to the back door."

"Gino's Bar is at the end of a strip center."

"Yes, I'm aware of the location."

"He's got a roof hatch."

"If it gets too hot, you go up to the roof and make your way to the last building, then climb your way down," Haley said.

"Wouldn't be the first time I had to do that," Recker said.

Jones raised his eyebrows as he continued working. "Yes, but let's hope that it was the last."

3

It wasn't long before Jones had pulled up a comprehensive file on Detective Andrews. The three men read over his information, but nothing stuck out that would make them apprehensive about the meeting. Other than being on Vincent's payroll, that is. But Andrews had a very good record, had been a detective for over ten years, and from what they could tell, wasn't a dirty cop. If they didn't already know he was in cahoots with Vincent, based on his record and file, they never would have looked twice at him.

"Seems like an upstanding cop," Haley said. "Nothing that would indicate he's not a trustworthy guy or anything."

"You mean, other than the fact he's a cop working with Vincent?" Recker asked.

Haley shook his head, agreeing with the point.

"Well, just because his record seems good, doesn't mean he's necessarily on the up and up," Jones said. "It could be he's just really good at covering his tracks and staying underneath the radar. We still must be cautious."

They continued preparing for the meeting, working right past dinner. Recker had forgotten he was supposed to go home for dinner with Mia. About six-thirty, Recker's phone started ringing again. When he went over to grab it, he made a grimacing face when he saw it was her.

"Hey."

"Hey, yourself," Mia said sternly, though she was just playing with him and wasn't really mad.

"So, how are you?"

"Good. You?"

"Good," Recker answered, thinking maybe she'd forgotten about dinner too. Or she just assumed something had come up and wasn't going to quiz him over it.

"Did you happen to forget something?" Mia asked, keeping up her angry front.

"Uh, yeah, I think so."

"You think? Or you know?"

Recker sighed, knowing he wasn't going to pull one over on her. "I'm sorry. I know I was supposed to come home for dinner. We just got caught up working on something."

"You know, I'm really getting tired of this," Mia

39

said, still in full acting mode. "If you're gonna keep on doing this, I just... I don't know if I can continue."

"Continue?" Recker asked, starting to get worried about what she was going to say. "You mean us?"

"Well... I mean, continue... this charade," she said, unable to keep up the front anymore and letting out a laugh. "I really had you going there for a moment, didn't I?"

A look of relief swept over Recker's face as he wiped some sweat off his forehead. "Yeah, yeah, you did."

"I'm sorry, sweetie, you're not really angry with me, are you?" Mia asked.

Recker thought for a moment, thinking it sounded like he might be getting off the hook for skipping dinner. "I guess that would depend on you."

"Me? Please don't be mad, honey, I was only joking with you."

"Well, how about we make a deal then?"

Mia wasn't sure she liked the sound of that. "What kind of deal?"

"I won't be mad at you for the kidding if you won't be mad at me for missing dinner," Recker said.

"I guess that's a deal I can live with."

Recker smiled. "OK, then."

"I get the better end of that deal."

"Oh yeah? How you figure?"

"Because I wasn't mad at you to begin with," Mia said.

"Oh," Recker replied, looking at the time. "I know I was supposed to be home around an hour ago. I hope you didn't have things waiting."

"No, actually I had to work a little late myself. I didn't get home until just a little while ago. Maybe ten or fifteen minutes."

"And you just felt the need to call and play a prank on me?"

Mia laughed. "It was kind of funny, don't you think?"

"Yeah, I almost fell on the floor laughing," Recker sarcastically said.

Mia figured they joked around long enough and changed the subject. "I take it you're not coming home anytime soon?"

"No, something really big came up."

"So, you're gonna make me eat alone again?"

"I'm sorry. I'll make it up to you."

"You better," Mia playfully said. "I miss you."

Recker looked over at his friends, not wanting to get too sappy and emotional in front of them and damage his dangerous reputation. He turned his head away from them and put his hand over his mouth as he talked more quietly.

"I miss you too."

Recker didn't talk quietly enough, though. Both Jones and Haley snapped their heads in his direction as he muttered the words, though they'd both heard him say such things before. Recker tried not to get overly sentimental in the work environment to keep his mind focused on business.

"Aww, I miss you too," Haley said, joking.

"Yes, we all miss you," Jones said, getting in on the gag.

Recker laughed to himself as he heard the pair behind him. He looked over at them, trying to give them a stern look to indicate his displeasure, but he couldn't pull it off. He waved his hand at them and turned his back to them again as he continued talking to his girlfriend.

"Was that David and Chris I heard?" Mia asked.

"Yeah, they apparently thought we needed an office clown or something."

"Tell them I said hi."

"I will."

"When will you be home?"

"Probably not till late," Recker answered. "Maybe eleven or twelve."

"That late?"

"I'm sorry. Something big came up."

"Such as?"

"Has to do with the police shootings."

"Shootings? I thought there was only one?" Mia asked.

"Another one happened this morning."

"Oh, no."

"Yeah, so we're gonna look into it."

"I don't get it. Why do you have to look into it? I'm

sure the police are launching their own investigation into it, aren't they?"

"Yeah, they are," Recker said. "But somebody asked if I could meet to talk about it."

"If someone has information, why would they talk to you instead of just going to the police about it?"

Recker cleared his throat, not really wanting to tell her who the meeting was with because he knew she'd worry. But, since he was trying not to keep secrets from her, decided to just spit it out. "It's a contact of Vincent's."

"OK? Still seems kind of sketchy to me."

Recker sighed. "You know, you're too smart for your own good sometimes."

"I know. Maybe it's a byproduct of being around you so much. You've rubbed off on me. I hardly ever take anything at face value anymore. There's usually always something else beneath the surface."

"OK, the person I'm meeting is a cop on Vincent's payroll. He asked Vincent to contact me and set something up."

"You're meeting a cop?" Mia asked, astonished. "There's so many ways that can go bad."

"I know. And we've been over every one of them. Vincent has assured me this is on the level."

"I mean no disrespect when I say this, and I know he's saved you before, but you do realize he's a criminal, right? And they're not always trustworthy people?"

"I know. We've been over it," Recker said again.

"OK. Well as long as you know."

"Don't worry. I'll be fine. Nothing will happen."

There was silence for a second as Mia thought of her reply, trying not to sound like the worried girlfriend, even though she was. "Is Chris going out with you when you meet this guy?"

"Yes. He's gonna be on the outside keeping a lookout. First sign of trouble, he'll let me know, and we'll be out of there. Does that make you feel better?"

"I guess a little bit."

"I promise, everything will be fine. If I even had the slightest bit of hesitation about this, I wouldn't go."

"OK. I trust your judgment."

"I'll get home as soon as I can," Recker said.

"I know. I'll wait up for you."

"You don't have to do that. I know you had a long day."

"It's fine. I don't like going to bed without you. I always get this... never mind... I probably shouldn't say anything."

"No, what?"

"When I go to bed without you, I get this weird feeling that I'll wake up and you still won't be there, and you won't be coming home. I dunno, it's stupid. Just some dumb nightmare that I have, I guess."

"It's not stupid."

"Yeah, well, I think I'm becoming more of a worrywart as I'm getting older," Mia said.

"I wouldn't want you to be any different than you are."

Recker didn't realize he had been speaking louder, the other two in the room clearly hearing what he was saying. And they weren't going to miss the opportunity to tease him some more.

"I wouldn't want you to be any different either," Jones said.

Haley also chimed in. "I love you just the way you are too."

Recker slowly turned his head toward the pair and tried to give them an evil stare, though it didn't stop them from making a few more sarcastic responses. After a few more minutes, Recker and Mia finally hung up. Recker put his phone in his pocket and walked over to the desk to get back to the meeting preparations.

"I wasn't aware we had the goof troop come into the office," Recker said.

Haley snickered, trying not to look at him.

"Yes, well, it's not every day we hear someone with your talents talking sweet nothings into his girlfriend's ear," Jones said.

"Sweet nothings? Really?" Recker asked. "OK, how about we stop talking about my love life and get back to business?"

"I'll concur with that."

The three men continued going over and perfecting their plans for the meeting for the next couple of hours until they were all comfortable with it. Once nine o'clock rolled around, Recker and Haley left the office. It was a little under a half hour drive to the bar and Recker wanted to get there early to scope the place out first. Gino's was a place he'd been to a few times before, so he was already familiar with the layout, but wanted to make sure he didn't spot any unfriendly people staking up a spot on the outside waiting for him to arrive.

Recker drove through the shopping center parking lot several times, both him and Haley looking for undercover police in the area. Neither could spot any, though. After they made their fifth pass without noticing any signs of potential trouble, Recker finally pulled into a parking spot. Before getting out, Recker and Haley made sure their communication devices were working and placed them inside their ears.

"First sign of trouble, you let me know," Recker said. "Even if you're not quite sure."

"I'll keep an eye out."

Recker then got out of the car and walked into the bar. There was a good-sized crowd inside, but it wasn't jam-packed. Recker looked around the place, just to make sure Detective Andrews didn't beat him there, and to see if he recognized anybody else that might give him pause. Andrews wasn't there yet, and nobody else made him jumpy, so he found a table in the middle of the room against the wall. He ordered a beer while he was waiting.

"Hey, handsome," a woman said.

Recker's eyes had been focused toward the door and didn't even notice the attractive brown-haired woman standing just to his right. He was a little unnerved as he sensed the woman out of the corner of his eye, looking at him. He slowly turned his head to look at her and gave her a smile.

"Is this seat taken?" the woman asked.

"Uh, I'm actually waiting for someone."

"Your girlfriend?"

"No, just a, uh, just a friend," Recker replied.

"Oh. Well, in that case, mind if I sit down and join you for a while?"

Haley had been carefully listening and spoke into Recker's ear. "Think she might be a cop?"

"Uh, no," Recker whispered.

"What was that?" the woman asked.

"Oh, uh, I was just saying I don't think that'd be a good idea."

"Why not?"

"Well, I have a girlfriend. I wouldn't exactly be too comfortable."

"Why not? Don't trust yourself?"

Recker wasn't sure what to say and didn't really want to keep the conversation going too much longer. He hated awkward situations like these. Though he was good at coercing confessions out of people, or questioning them about their behavior, some things he wasn't as proficient at. Fending an interested and flirty woman away from him would definitely classify as something he wasn't entirely comfortable with. She wasn't an unattractive woman, but considering he already had the most amazing woman at home waiting for him, and he was there on business and waiting for his contact, it wasn't a proposition he was particularly interested in.

Recker looked up at her and smiled. "Maybe another time."

The woman shrugged and grabbed a napkin off the table. She pulled a pen out of the pocket of her jeans and leaned on the table, trying to give Recker an ample view of her cleavage through her low-cut top. Recker caught a quick glimpse of her chest before he realized what she was trying to do and cleared his throat and raised his eyebrows as he looked over toward the door, not wanting to view her assets. Out of the corner of his eye, he saw she was finished and standing straight again and he turned his head to look at her again.

"If you ever decide to change your mind, give me a call," the woman said, giving him a smile.

Recker nodded. "I'll do that."

The woman walked away, taking a quick peek back at him, hoping he'd be glancing at her in her tightly-worn jeans. He wasn't, though. If he was single, maybe he'd have given her a second look. But not with Mia. Recker thought it was inappropriate and disrespectful to be looking at other women, even if it was just in passing or for a quick second. He wasn't interested in playing around, or seeing what else was out there, or even just looking for fun.

"Did, uh, what I think happen... happen?" Haley asked, breaking up the silence.

Recker coughed, putting his hand over his mouth. "Yep. Sure did."

Haley laughed. "You sounded like a fish out of water."

"That type of stuff is definitely not my scene."

"You gonna call her later?"

"Are you crazy?" Recker asked. "I'd have to be an idiot to do that to Mia."

"I agree. Just checking."

"You want the number? You can have it. I'll save it for you."

"I think she might ask questions about how I'd have it," Haley said.

Recker looked over to see where the woman was, watching her standing by the bar, talking to another man. "Something tells me that I'm not the only one she's tried that with. She probably doesn't even remember everyone she's handed her number out to."

"Well, hopefully we can get you out of there soon to save yourself."

"You and me both. I think I'd rather have ten hit men walk through that door and attempt to kill me than have to deal with that type of conversation again," Recker said.

"I dunno, you seemed to have done all right with

Mia. You can't be too bad."

"That was kind of an accident. And it happened naturally. If one of us went up to the other in a bar and started talking, who knows how it would have turned out? Maybe we would have never talked again."

"From the way I hear it, that's kind of how it happened, isn't it?" Haley asked.

"Not quite like that. It wasn't anything where one of us went up to the other and started flirting. She came up to me in a diner after spotting me tailing her. A slightly different circumstance."

"I don't know. You two seem perfect for each other. I'd like to think that somehow you two would have found each other no matter what."

"What? Like fate or something?"

"Yeah, something like that," Haley said. "Despite the business we're in, I'd like to think that not everything is left purely to chance. I'd like to think some things are just meant to be. Maybe I'm a hopeless romantic."

"Yeah, well, I'll leave all that kind of stuff to you," Recker said with a laugh. "How's everything looking out there?"

"Quiet. Not seeing anything out here unusual. The bar's open later than everything else in here and some cars are starting to leave, so most of the cars here are probably people inside the bar."

"That'll make it a little easier to identify trouble."

Five minutes to ten, Haley saw a white car pull into

the shopping center and park in front of the bar. He kept his eyes glued to the car and a few seconds after the ignition shut off, a man got out from the driver side. Haley looked at the picture of Andrews on his phone and compared it to the driver. It was a match.

"Mike, Andrews just pulled in. He's walking in now."

"Got it. Any signs that he brought friends?"

"Negative."

"All right, keep a lookout."

Detective Andrews walked into the bar and looked around, not sure how he was going to recognize the man he was meeting. Vincent had assured him that Recker would find him once he entered the bar. He just stood there for a minute, trying to keep himself in plain sight to be recognized. Recker thought the detective looked a little nervous. It wasn't a particularly warm, muggy night, so he assumed the sweat on Andrews' forehead was due to his nerves. Recker then stood and waited for Andrews to lock eyes on him. Once their eyes focused on each other, Recker gave the detective a subtle nod. Andrews walked over to Recker's table and stood in front of him.

Andrews pointed at the chair, not wanting to assume anything with the famous vigilante. "You mind?"

Recker shook his head. "Go ahead."

Andrews pulled the chair out and sat across from him. He clasped his hands and fiddled with his fingers as he began speaking. "I guess I should say thanks for agreeing to do this. I know you must've had some reservations about it."

"I did."

"I figured as much. I just want you to know right off the bat there's no tricks involved or anything."

Recker nodded to let him know he understood. "So, what did you wanna talk about?"

Andrews looked around and wiped his forehead, still looking nervous.

"Looking for somebody?" Recker asked.

"No. Sorry. I guess I'm just a little nervous here."

"Why?"

"I'm a cop. You're a wanted man. We make strange bedfellows, no?"

"Is that any different than you working for Vincent?"

"That's a little different," Andrews answered.

"How you figure?"

"He flies a little bit underneath the radar more than you do. You've almost become a larger-than-life figure in this town. Seventy percent of the boys on the force wanna give you a medal and erect a statue in your honor."

"And the other thirty percent wanna lock me up?" Recker asked.

Andrews tilted his head and made a face.

"So which side do you fall on?"

"Listen, from what I can tell, you've never hurt an

innocent person and only have targeted criminals. Plus, there was that business with Bernal a while back where you prevented a cop from getting shot. From where I stand, that puts us on the same side."

"Good to know."

"Hey, if I ever roll up on a crime scene and you're still there, you can keep on walking as far as I'm concerned," Andrews said.

"I'll keep that in mind."

"As far as working with Vincent, that's something that just kind of happened," Andrews said, looking away and making a face, indicating that he wasn't very proud of it. "My wife got really sick, had cancer, medical bills really started piling up, couldn't afford payments on the house, just got deeper and deeper in debt."

"And you reached out to him?"

Andrews laughed, almost not believing himself how it went down. "No, not quite. I was working a case that involved Jimmy Malloy, Vincent's right-hand man."

"I know him."

"One day, Vincent approached me as I was eating lunch at a diner, offered me a deal."

"What kind of deal?" Recker asked.

"To let another one of his boys take the rap instead of Malloy. In exchange for that, and for providing information that he might need periodically, he gives me a little something every month."

Recker nodded, sympathetic to the man's story. "Must come in handy."

"It does. I wanna make it clear, though, that I'm not a dirty cop. I don't do anything illegal, well, outside of that I guess. But I love my job, I love this city, and I love helping people. If it came down to helping Vincent or helping another cop, I'd choose the cop all day, every day. A hundred percent."

"What exactly do you do for him now?"

"He has certain business interests all over the place. If I ever get wind of anything that involves those interests, or any of his men, I let him know. That's all. I know, you're probably thinking I'm a hypocrite, but the reasoning is sound on my end."

Recker shrugged. "Who am I to say you're wrong? We all have to have a justification for what we do."

Andrews let out a laugh, agreeing with his point. "Yeah. I have to say, you're not quite what I was expecting."

"Oh? What were you expecting?"

"I dunno. I mean, I've seen your face before, you know, with it being plastered on the news and all. But you seem like a normal, regular guy just sitting here. You see and hear news stories about you and your work and I guess I kind of expected someone that's... I dunno, a lot different. Like one of those old-time movie gangsters that's just mean and nasty and wants to shoot someone on sight."

"Well, I guess people rarely live up to expectations," Recker said.

"Only personality wise. Your work still speaks for itself."

"Thanks. I guess we should stop talking about ourselves here and get down to business."

"Yeah. I guess you've heard about the two police shootings by now?" Andrews asked.

"I have."

"You don't happen to have any info on it, do you?"

"No. I didn't even find out about the first one until this morning," Recker answered.

"Yeah, they did a good job of keeping it out of the news."

"Is that what you wanted me for? To see if I knew of anything?"

"Well, partially. I'm actually one of the detectives who's been assigned to work the cases, along with four other guys."

"And you want me to help?" Recker asked.

"I know you got your own way of doing things. You've got some system perfected that you can find things out about people. In some ways, you're probably better at finding stuff than we are."

Recker smiled. "I won't argue there."

"Yeah, well, if you could keep an ear out and if you turn anything, maybe give me a shout?"

Though Recker wasn't against doing as the detective

asked, something wasn't making sense to him. It was still very early in the investigation period. The fact Andrews was already asking for help seemed a little strange. If it had been a few weeks or a month, and the police weren't making any headway, Recker might have understood reaching out to him. But the second shooting just occurred that morning. It was way too soon in his mind to be asking for help from someone who wasn't considered on the same side of the law. It reeked of being a desperation move. One that didn't need to occur just yet.

"You'll have to forgive me for being a little skeptical, but isn't a little soon to be asking for help from me?" Recker asked.

"What do you mean?"

"The first shooting just happened a couple days ago. The second this morning. I mean, that's hardly enough time to just get the facts of what happened written in your notebook, isn't it?"

Andrews moved his head around and sighed, looking at various people in the bar. Recker could tell by his face he was holding something back. Andrews then ordered a beer, figuring he could use a little something extra in his system to help explain things.

"I guess that's why you're as good as you are, huh?" Andrews asked.

"I'm good at reading people."

"So I see. All right, so look, these aren't the first two shootings that we've attributed to this guy."

"How many more?"

"The first one that we think he did was a couple weeks ago. The victim was a low-level drug dealer."

Recker looked at him strangely, not seeing the connection to a minor drug player and two police officers. "So how you figure they're related?"

Andrews took a sip of his beer. "Well, it gets a little more complicated than just that. First, he was killed with a forty-five hollow-point bullet."

"Not really what you would call conclusive evidence."

"No, but there's more. Then last week, another guy dropped dead, courtesy of a forty-five hollow-point bullet."

"What was his line of work?" Recker asked, assuming it was something illegal.

"That's just it. He wasn't a criminal. He was just a regular guy."

"Then how does it fit?"

"Apparently, this guy rode his bike to and from work every night. Same route every time. About five days after the drug dealer went down. And the path that he rode every night, was the very same area that the drug dealer frequented. Matter of fact, they were killed one street apart from each other," Andrews said.

"That is a pretty big coincidence."

"Yeah. So, we're figuring that maybe the guy saw a transaction go down, something he wasn't supposed to see, and he got taken out for it."

"Question the guy's family or anything? Maybe he told someone what he saw," Recker said.

"Ahh, we checked. He was a young kid, about twenty-two, still lived with his mother and younger sister. They didn't know anything about it. I doubt he would've told them anything and bogged them down with that kind of stuff."

"That's fine, but I still don't see how that relates to the two officers getting shot."

"The first officer that got shot was Anthony Rios. He's a seven-year veteran on an undercover assignment. Guess how he figures into this?"

"He was buying off the drug dealer?"

Andrews nodded. "Bingo. Guess where he was shot?"

"Same area."

"Same street as the drug dealer."

"What was his name?" Recker asked.

"Kevin Maldonado."

"What was Rios' assignment?"

"To get in close with Maldonado and figure out where he's getting his stash from. He was a name we started hearing more from, moving up the ladder, you know what I mean?"

"I think so."

"We think there might be an emerging drug player in the city and we believed Maldonado had ties to him."

"What about the cop this morning?"

Andrews threw his hand up and looked disgusted as his eyes glanced around the room. "That we don't know. We haven't figured out yet how that comes into play."

"No ties to any of them?" Recker asked.

"Not that we've uncovered so far. Rios was in a narcotics unit. The officer that got shot this morning was Peter Kirby. He works in a patrol unit. As far as we can tell, he hasn't had any interaction with Rios or Maldonado."

"And you're sure it's the same shooter?"

"Same type of bullet, same markings. We're pretty sure it's the same guy."

"And you don't have any other leads or suspects?"

"Not yet, no," Andrews answered, shaking his head.

"How about something in their personal life? Maybe the answer lies there, and they killed the drug dealer and other guy to make it look like it's something else."

"Well, we obviously haven't been able to check out everything with Kirby yet since it's still fresh. Rios, though, nothing turned up adversarial."

"And nobody on the street knows anything?" Recker asked.

"Not so far."

"Did you check with Vincent to see if he knows anything?"

"No."

"Why not?"

"You may not believe this, but I try to keep my conversations with him limited. I don't want to ask him favors that I might have to repay later," Andrews said.

"What is it that you're actually asking me to do?"

"Poke around a little, see what you can dig up. I dunno, maybe we're missing something, maybe something got overlooked."

"Seems a little weird that you're here asking this of me," Recker said. "Seems like you'd have the whole department and then some at your disposal for this."

"Well, you're right there, but when you don't have any leads or suspects to work off, you get desperate pretty quick. Especially when it's cops that start falling. And believe me, they're the only reason I'm even here. If it was just a bunch of criminals getting whacked, I wouldn't be here either."

"You think there might be more to come?"

Andrews sighed. "I don't know. I hope not. But, something's telling me there's gonna be more if we don't wrap this up quick. And I'd make a deal with just about anyone to make sure no other cops get it."

"Rios is still alive, though, right?"

"Yeah, was released yesterday and pulled off the undercover assignment this morning."

"He doesn't have any ideas?"

"None. He's as in the dark as the rest of us."

"And if I actually make headway on this?" Recker asked. "What is it that you want me to do? Wrap him up in a bow for you?"

"I guess that depends on what the situation calls for. If there's any way that you can let me know so I can take him in, I'd appreciate getting a heads up on it. If it's a situation where your life is on the line and you gotta take him down, then you gotta do what you gotta do. If that's the case, I'd still appreciate it if you could let me know so I can wrap the case up."

Recker had all the information he needed at that point and wanted to start winding things down. He didn't want to sit there too long and make himself a target, just in case. He was pretty sure Andrews was leveling with him about everything. He didn't get any sense the detective was trying to mislead him or manipulate him in any way.

"All right, I think I've got enough to start with," Recker said.

"Does that mean you're on it?"

"I'll see what I can find out."

A relieved look came across Andrews' face and he broke out a smile. "Just so we're clear on everything, I can't offer you money or anything for this."

"It's fine. I'm not interested in money."

"OK, well, if there's anything I can ever do for you, just name it. Within reason. I can't get you out of jail or anything if you ever get brought in. Maybe I can help you avoid that if I ever hear someone's on the verge of nailing you, though."

"I'll remember that."

"Well, thanks a lot. Really appreciate this," Andrews said.

He hesitated for a second, not sure whether he should put his hand out and offer to shake Recker's. He didn't know if the man known as The Silencer would be all that interested in shaking the hand of a police officer. Andrews finally stuck his hand out, nervous about the response, hoping he wouldn't just get blown off. Recker, after a brief hesitation himself, put his hand out to finish the handshake. Andrews got up to leave, before remembering a few final questions.

"Oh, uh, do you have a name or something to call you?" Andrews asked. "Kind of weird just calling you Silencer, you know?"

Recker wasn't sure it was in his best interests to reveal any part of his name, but then figured why not? It was an alias, anyway, and even if Andrews decided to run it through his computers, it wouldn't come back with anything. There was really no harm in him knowing his name.

"Mike."

"One final thing," Andrews said. "How can I reach you or get in touch if I have something else for you or if you find out anything?"

"I got your number."

"You do? How?"

"Like you said earlier... I've got my ways."

4

R ecker stayed seated as Andrews left the bar. He alerted Haley the detective was on his way out and for him to keep an eye on him. Andrews immediately got in his car and pulled out of the parking lot. As soon as he did, Haley let Recker know.

"Mike, Andrews is gone."

"See anything out there?"

"No, quiet as it was before."

"Did he get on his phone or anything as he walked to the car?" Recker asked.

"No. Didn't do anything suspicious. Went right to his car and left right away."

"All right, good. Pull around to the back door and pick me up."

"You got it. On my way."

Recker got up from his table and walked over to the

bar. The bartender on duty that night was also the owner of the place.

"Charlie, you mind if I go out the back?" Recker asked.

"Yeah, no problem, let me just open it up for you."

Two years earlier, Recker saved Charlie from getting robbed. From that night on, Charlie let Recker know if he ever needed anything, to let him know. Recker took him up on that and used his bar a few times for meeting purposes. Charlie was always very grateful for The Silencer in helping and saving him that he never breathed a word about him occasionally showing up. He always felt better, and safer, when Recker stopped by periodically and he was happy to help him out in whatever way he needed. Even if it was just the use of a table for an hour or two.

"How was your meeting?" Charlie asked, as the two walked to the back door.

"Went fine, thanks."

"Good. Glad to hear it."

"Thanks for letting me use your place," Recker said, patting him on the shoulder.

"Oh, no problem, champ. Anytime you ever need it, just say the word, you know that."

Charlie unlocked the back door and opened it a sliver before closing it quickly.

"You want me to peek out there just to make sure there's no shenanigans out there?"

Recker smiled, appreciating the gesture. "No, I think it's OK."

"Well OK, if you say so."

Charlie opened the door again, and the two shook hands before Recker walked out. Haley had the SUV parked only a few feet away so Recker hopped in the passenger seat. As the car started to drive away, Charlie gave the pair a wave goodbye, though he didn't know who the driver was.

"You know that guy?" Haley asked.

"Yeah. He owns the bar."

"I think he recognized me."

"No, you're good."

"You trust him?"

"Hmm?" Recker asked, staring out the window. "Oh, yeah. He's fine. I stopped a robbery here last year. He told me if I ever needed to use his place for anything to just say the word."

"Oh. Good deal."

"Yeah, I've used the place a few times. He's trustworthy. Even if he sees you, he won't say anything."

As they drove back to the office, they talked about the specifics of the meeting.

"What'd you think?" Haley asked. "Think he's on the level?"

Recker nodded. "Yeah. I think he is."

"Still seems weird to me."

"Certainly isn't normal," Recker said.

"You think he was holding something else back?"

"Why? You think so?"

"I dunno. I guess I'm just having a hard time getting a grasp on this."

"I think he's afraid more bodies are gonna drop before they find out who it is and is just trying to prevent it as much as possible."

"Yeah, I guess so."

They continued tossing questions back and forth with each other as they discussed the situation, each coming up with some ideas as to what might have been going on. Once they got back to the office, all the lights were still on as Jones was banging away at the computer keyboard. As soon as he heard the two of them enter, he swiveled his chair around to greet them. He looked the two of them over as they walked closer to him.

"I don't see any holes," Jones quipped.

"They had bad aim," Recker shot back.

Jones looked to Haley for the straight story. Though they hadn't reported running into any trouble, Jones couldn't always tell when Recker was joking. Even when he was in a gunfight, he sometimes played it off as if it was no big deal. So the times he said he wasn't, but made a joke referencing it, Jones sometimes looked at him cross-eyed.

Haley shook his head. "There was no trouble."

"Let's keep this short," Recker said, grabbing a chair, and sitting. "Mia's waiting up for me."

"Let's get to the gist of things then, shall we?" Jones asked. "Your thoughts from the meeting?"

"He seemed like he was legit. I didn't get any bad vibes or think he was trying to pull the rug out from under me."

"What exactly did he want?"

Recker shrugged. "Seemed like he just wanted help if we could give it."

"And that's all there was to it?"

"Well, not quite. He did reveal that there have been more than two shootings that they attribute to this shooter."

"Oh?" Jones said, looking confused. "I didn't hear of anything else."

"The other two victims weren't cops. One was a drug dealer, and the other was an innocent person who they think may have been a witness to something."

"Witness to what?"

"Don't know. But the undercover cop, the drug dealer, and the witness, were all shot in the same area. Two on the same street, the other on the next street over."

Jones ran his fingers over his mouth, deep in thought. "Now that is interesting, isn't it?"

"The police don't seem to have any leads or suspects," Recker said. "I think they're just worried, at least Andrews is, that more bodies are gonna drop soon before they get a beat on whoever it is."

"I guess they're just trying to throw their nets out as wide as possible in hopes of catching something."

Recker threw his hands up. "Guess so."

"Did he give you any other details, files, anything we can use to start looking into it?"

"No. What do we need that for? Since when couldn't we find out whatever we needed on our own?"

"Good point. I just thought it might be a little quicker," Jones replied.

Recker stood, ready to call it a night. "Well, I guess we can get started on it in the morning."

"Well, at some point tomorrow, anyway."

"What do you mean?"

"Have you forgotten we have other things to attend to?" Jones asked. "We're not here to serve at the whim of the police department. I told you earlier that we were close to working on another case of our own."

"Guess we'll be pulling down double duty."

"Is it something that requires both of us?" Haley asked. "Maybe I can take the case and Mike sticks on the police thing?"

"We'll discuss it more tomorrow," Jones said. "As I said, we'll handle our own business first. As much as I respect the police and don't wish any harm to come to them, they do have their own investigation capabilities."

Recker seemed indifferent. He certainly wasn't against helping the police out, but understood Jones' point of view.

"How bad is this upcoming case?" Recker asked.

"It looks as though it could be quite severe," Jones answered.

"How soon is the threat level?"

"Could be tomorrow. Possibly the day after. I have not nailed down a definitive time frame yet."

"You haven't nailed it down or they haven't figured it out yet?"

"They have not said specifically yet."

"All right. Well, I guess we'll figure all that out tomorrow."

The three men then went their separate ways for the night. Jones stayed up for another hour to work some more, while Recker and Haley went to their respective apartments. Just as she promised, Mia was up and watching TV to pass the time as she waited for Recker to get home. As soon as he did, she rushed over to him and threw her arms around him as they passionately embraced for a minute or two.

"I take it everything went well tonight?" Mia asked.

"Just like I told you it would."

"I know. I'm sorry for worrying."

"It's fine," Recker replied with a kiss.

Mia helped him take his coat off and walked over to the closet to hang it up. As soon as she put it on the hanger, she put her hands inside the pockets to make sure there was nothing in there Recker might need. She pulled out a piece of paper and saw a woman's name and phone number written on it. Slightly alarmed, though not terribly so, as she was sure he had a good explanation for it, Mia closed the closet door and started walking toward the couch where Recker was now sitting.

"Would you like to explain what this is?" Mia asked, holding the napkin up in the air between two of her fingers.

Recker squinted for a second, not sure what it was. He quickly realized what it was and batted his eyes. He was a little mad at himself for not ditching it or giving it to Haley. He had completely forgotten about the woman who gave him her phone number. As she waited for an explanation, Mia put her hands on her hips, giving off a vibe that she was either annoyed, jealous, or both. In reality, she was sure there was a logical reason behind it. She trusted him completely and didn't give the tiniest thought to him ever cheating on her. But she liked to have a little fun with him sometimes.

"Oh, that," Recker said.

"Yeah, this."

"Well, there's a funny story behind that."

Mia made a huge fake smile. "I'll bet."

Recker laughed. "No, really. I was sitting at a table in the bar waiting for my contact to show up and this woman walked up to me and gave it to me."

"And you just conveniently put it in your pocket?" Mia asked.

Recker faked a cough as he cleared his throat.

"Well, I was actually going to give it to Chris to see if he wanted to call the girl up or something."

"Oh. Because you just love to play Suzy Matchmaker now? You're just an old-fashioned romantic at heart and want all your friends to be healthy and happily in love for the rest of their lives?"

Recker couldn't help but let out a smile at the reference. He was sure he'd never be called Suzy Matchmaker again. But it was kind of amusing. "Uh, yeah, something like that. I figured if I'm gonna be lucky enough to find the woman I'd like to spend the rest of my life with, why shouldn't everyone else?"

This time, it was Mia with the smile. "Good save. You know, you're becoming much more of a smooth talker."

Recker didn't really have a comeback and just shrugged. "Honest. It's exactly the way it happened."

Mia slowly marched over to him, trying to keep her mad face plastered on, though she was having a tough time accomplishing it. Once she reached the couch, she leaned over and planted a kiss on Recker's lips.

"Of course I believe you. Looked like you were starting to sweat there for a second, though," she said with a smile.

"Eh, not really. I would hope that you know it would take a lot more than some girl in a bar to take me away from you."

Mia faked another offended look. "A lot more? It better be darn near impossible."

"Well, I don't want you to get too comfortable," Recker joked.

Mia raised her eyebrows and looked at him sternly, still playing around with him. "You wanna say that again?"

"Maybe I should just quit while I'm ahead."

Mia nodded. "That might be a good idea."

Mia leaned in and put her hands on the back of Recker's head, giving him a kiss on the forehead, then another kiss on the lips. "I love you," she said.

"I love you too," Recker replied.

Mia then stood straight and looked at the napkin for a moment. "So, what should I do with this? Put it back in your pocket? Give it to Chris? Throw it out?"

"Might as well just throw it out."

"Why? Don't you think Chris will want it?"

"Well, considering that woman seemed to be going to just about every guy there who looked like he was alone, I don't think she'd be his type."

Mia gave him a disappointed look. "Mike, don't assume she's that type of girl. Maybe she was just lonely and looking for someone. Doesn't mean she was ready to go home with every man she came into contact with."

"You're right. I shouldn't assume."

"Was she pushy or anything?"

Recker shook his head. "No, not really. Ahh, just throw it out. Chris can get his own girls. I did."

Mia walked into the kitchen and tossed the napkin into the trash can.

"I think I'll just get ready for bed," she said, walking past him and into their bedroom.

Recker sighed. "Yeah, probably a good idea."

After just a couple minutes, she opened the door and stood within the framework, wearing nothing but a baseball jersey that just barely covered all her essentials.

"Would you care to join me?" she seductively asked.

"Yeah, I think I would."

"Unless you're too tired or something."

Recker got up and hurried into the bedroom. "Not that tired."

5

---

ecker, Jones, and Haley met up in the office just after eight. They had a quick breakfast before they started discussing business and making plans for the day. They all sat at the desk as Jones started going over their next case.

"You have things nailed down yet?" Recker asked.

Jones sighed and looked at the computer screen, usually a sign there was something he didn't like in what he was about to say. "Not totally. And unfortunately, we're going to have to roll without having the full plan in play."

"What do you mean?"

"Well, I know the players involved. I know the general basics of the scheme. I just don't know how it will all unfold."

"What's going on?" Haley asked.

Jones gave each of the Silencers a folder with all

the particulars, each getting the same exact information. It was easier that way, instead of them passing papers around back and forth.

"As you can see, this may get very deeply involved," Jones said.

As Recker looked at the information, his eyes shifted around, and a deeply concerned look fell over his face. "The victim's a six-month-old baby girl?"

"Well, Kathrynn Rocco is the target. I believe she is not what this group of kidnappers is really after though."

"Not a ransom attempt?"

"Hardly."

"Her mother is Judge Sandra Rocco?" Haley said.

"Yes," Jones said, pointing at him. "And that's where it gets interesting. Judge Rocco is about to preside over a high-profile trial involving a criminal defense attorney who was arrested over some shady dealings he had."

"When's this trial start?" Recker asked.

"Three days from now."

"So, they're gonna kidnap the child in hopes of swaying her decisions?"

"I would think that's the play."

"So, they're just gonna hold this kid until the trial's over?" Haley asked.

"It looks like that's the plan," Jones replied.

"So how are they gonna do it?"

"Well, Judge Rocco has a nanny that cares for the

child during the day. From what I can gather, she takes the baby for a walk every day unless it rains."

"And on a set schedule," Recker said, looking disturbed.

"Almost like clockwork. She takes the baby to Rittenhouse Square Park at one o'clock every day."

"Why not just put a sign on the kid that says kidnap me?"

Jones could understand his friend's frustration, though he tried to limit it. "Mike, not everyone is as alert to these things as we are. You can't always blame people for not thinking like us."

Recker nodded. "I know. I just... it just bothers me when a kid is involved."

"I know. And we'll do everything we can to protect her."

"The nanny isn't in on it, is she?"

"No. She's a twenty-five-year-old that's apparently known the judge for six years, since she was in college. There doesn't appear to be any connection."

Haley scratched the top of his head as he read the information in the folder. "If there's been any threats, why isn't the judge and her family under protection? U.S. Marshals should be involved, shouldn't they?"

"They would be if there was a threat levied," Jones replied. "The problem is, there hasn't been any."

"They haven't made any threats against the judge?"

"None whatsoever. The good judge has no idea

what they're planning or even that there's any kind of threat at all."

"So how many people are involved in this?" Recker asked.

"That's a little tougher to determine right now. I know three definitely, but I suspect there's more."

"Why do you think that?"

"Some of the messages they've sent each other indicated there was at least one or two more," Jones said. "Now, perhaps they were speaking in code, or just being cautious, but several emails I intercepted seemed to suggest another man that they reported to."

"So, what exactly is their plan?" Haley asked. "I mean, they have to have something other than just snatching the kid in broad daylight."

"Chris is right," Recker said. "Rittenhouse Park isn't exactly an off the beaten path area. There's a good number of people there. If they just take the kid out in the open, they're gonna draw a lot of attention to themselves."

"Unfortunately, that's all the information I have right now. I don't yet know how they're going to do it. I just know that they will," Jones said.

The trio fell silent for a minute, all of whom were thinking about the situation. "They're going to need an elaborate setup," Recker said.

"They're probably gonna have a car already running nearby that they can jump into," Haley said.

"So, assuming they're not just gonna walk up to the

nanny and take the kid from her and run, they're going to have some sort of distraction."

"That would seem to be the most likely scenario," Jones said. "But that also leads us up to problem number two."

"Which is?"

"I still haven't pinned down the date this is happening."

"You mean you still don't know?" Recker asked. "I was under the impression this was going down today."

"It very well could be today."

"Or not?"

"Or not," Jones replied. "Either they're using code phrases to disguise the date, or they just have not set a timetable yet."

"Or there's a third option."

"Which is?"

"That they have set a date and you just haven't gotten it yet," Recker said.

"Yes, it is possible that they may have met off channel."

"So, what are we gonna do?" Haley asked.

Recker sighed, not really liking the only choice available, though he knew there was nothing else they could do. "Looks like we're gonna be taking a walk in the park."

"For how long?"

"Until someone shows up," Recker replied.

"How positive are we that it's actually gonna go down in the park?"

"I'm quite certain, why do you ask? Do you have another idea?" Jones said.

"Well, knowing that it might be busy in the park, could it happen somewhere else? Maybe on the street walking to the park or on the way back?"

"The judge lives within walking distance of the park so I guess it is theoretically possible it could happen on the way there. But all the information that I could piece together indicated that it would be done in the park."

"Probably would be a good idea if one of us had eyes on the kid as soon as they leave the judge's house," Recker said.

"As long as you keep your distance."

"Why?"

"If you're too close, and the kidnappers also have their eyes on the nanny from the moment she leaves the house, then it's quite possible they'll spot and notice you," Jones said. "Could blow your cover sky-high."

"Might be a chance we have to take. Even if we're spotted, might be enough to scare them off."

"I don't think so."

"Why not?"

"Because we now know that these people are targeting the judge," Jones said. "We know what they're planning and can act accordingly. If we play this right, we can foil the plot, and disable the perpetrators."

"Alive?"

"That is my hope. If they're alive and arrested, they can be questioned, then perhaps it will be learned how far up the chain it goes and whether it was in fact ordered by our shady lawyer friend. But if we spoil the plan too soon, then there's no telling whether they'll try to strike again, whether they'll abandon this plan and try something different, or whether we'll even learn of the new plan at all. That is a lot to leave up to chance, don't you think?"

Recker nodded, agreeing with the professor's thoughts. "That is a lot to leave up to chance. All right, we'll just have to stake the park out every day until the thing goes down."

"What about the police problem?" Haley asked.

Recker looked at Jones, deferring the question to him.

"I will begin to look into it today," Jones said. "I don't know how much I'll be able to uncover, though. I'm much better at discovering problems before they happen than after the fact. Besides that, it's not like we have much to work with. We don't really have much in the way of information or evidence that would point us in any specific direction."

"Maybe we need some extra eyes and ears in the field," Recker said.

"And by that you mean?"

"Tyrell."

"Mike, as good as Tyrell is, and he is quite good at finding and getting information, don't you think the police have their own contacts on the street? I mean, I'm sure they have their own Tyrell's."

"Maybe so. But I would put money on ours over theirs."

"As you wish."

Recker took out his phone and called Tyrell's number. In the time since Jeremiah was killed, Tyrell had not been as active on the streets. He still did some occasional jobs for Vincent, as well as whenever Recker needed something, but his other activities had been cut down. He was still making as much money, if not more, than he was with Jeremiah. Recker usually had a need for him at least a couple of times every month and he always made sure Tyrell was well compensated.

Recker probably gave Tyrell more money than was necessary, but he wanted to make sure Tyrell wasn't short on what he needed. Mostly because he didn't want Tyrell branching off and trying other things that were more dangerous and risk the possibility of getting arrested. Part of it was because they were friends. The other part was because they'd spent the last several years cultivating a relationship that ran like a finely tuned vintage car. If Tyrell got himself jammed up, then Recker would be left without a guy on the street who could get the information that he did. Either that, or he'd have to try to find someone new. And Recker wasn't much interested in that scenario. It took time for Recker to trust new people. He already knew what Tyrell could do, he knew he could be trusted.

"Yo, what's up?" Tyrell greeted.

"Hey, have some work for you."

"Whatcha got?"

"You know anything about those police shootings?" Recker asked.

"Nah, not really."

"Do you know about them though?"

"I heard a cop got shot this morning. That's about it though."

"Well, it goes a little deeper than that."

"Usually does."

"I want you to start digging your nose into it and see what you can find out. There's been one uniformed officer shot, one undercover cop, a drug dealer, and what appears to be a possible witness."

"All right, I'll see what I can do," Tyrell said. "What kind of time frame are you looking at?"

"As soon as possible. No telling when the shooter will strike again."

"OK, no sweat. Why you involved with this, though? Not really your MO."

"Let's just say someone on the inside is concerned and wants as much help as possible to put an end to this quickly."

"All right, you got it, man. I'll start now. Send me an

email with as much as you got on it."

"I will. I'll have David do it in a few minutes. I'm on my way to something else right now."

After they hung up, Recker instructed Jones to send the email to Tyrell as he asked. They still had some time before they had to go to the park, so they spent every bit of it going over the layout of the park and where each of them would be.

"Let's go over the people we know are involved in this," Recker said.

They started studying the sheets of information that Jones had compiled on the people he had identified as being a part of the caper. As they began going over it, Recker's phone rang.

"You sure are popular this morning," Jones said.

Recker pulled out his phone again, surprised that Malloy would be calling him.

"Yeah?" Recker answered.

"You free to talk for a few minutes?" Malloy asked.

"Yeah, I guess so."

"Good. Boss wants to talk to you, hold on."

"Mike, how are you?" Vincent asked.

"OK. You?"

"Not too bad considering."

"So, what's up?" Recker asked.

"Just wondering how your meeting with our mutual friend went last night?"

"It went fine."

"Good. I take it everything was on the up and up

like I said. That's part of why I called, just wanted to make sure I wasn't made a liar out of."

"No, everything went down without a hitch."

"Glad to hear it."

"Do you plan on giving our friend a hand?" Vincent asked.

"I'll see what I can do. I'm not making any promises. I've got other stuff I need to work on, but if I learn anything, I'll pass it along."

"That's fine. It helps you in the long run, anyway."

"How's that?" Recker asked.

"The more people you know in places of authority, the more chances are that you'll get help when you need it the most."

"I don't do things with the expectation of someone owing me a favor later."

"Of course not," Vincent said. "But it doesn't hurt to know people. Especially people such as us who aren't exactly known for being on the right side of the law."

"I suppose not. I take it that since he came to me for assistance that you don't have any ideas yourself as to who's behind it?"

"I do not. If I did, I'd serve the shooter up on a silver platter myself. This kind of behavior is bad for business."

"I guess this type of stuff is bad for everyone, huh?"

"Yes, it is. Brings too much heat, too much scrutiny, too much publicity and public pressure. Bad for all of us."

"I guess that means it's fairly safe to assume that it's nobody involved in your organization?" Recker said.

"Nobody involved in my organization would dare do something like that. Even if they're only occasionally employed by me. Something like that would have to be authorized by me personally. If someone did that without my knowledge and consent, they would be dealt with severely."

The two men continued talking for a few more minutes, neither saying anything more than what was already said. As far as Recker could tell, Vincent's main concern seemed to be that no nefarious behavior went down. Though many people had differing opinions of the crime boss, and most of them would probably be accurate, Vincent did strive to be a man of his word, especially to those people he respected or worked with. And Recker qualified on both counts.

"Anything we need to be concerned about?" Jones asked, since he knew Vincent usually didn't call just to shoot the breeze.

"No. I think he just wanted to make sure I wasn't in jail."

"Huh?"

"From last night. Meeting the detective. I think he just wanted to make sure I wasn't set up," Recker said.

"Oh. Well how nice of him to be concerned about your welfare."

"Yeah. Enough about him. Let's get back to business."

6

It was eleven o'clock, and Recker and Haley were getting ready to leave. Before they left, they all went over the information and plan one more time with Jones. There were three men they knew were involved. All of whom had criminal records. Recker was almost positive there would be more, though. The three men they were aware of had all worked together previously. They weren't known to work with anyone else, but something was gnawing at him that there had to be more. He figured if they were to pull something like this off, they had to at least have six or eight people working it. Of course, he hoped he was wrong, and there were only the three. The fewer people he had to deal with, the better he liked it. As Recker and Haley were about to leave the office, Jones had some last-minute advice for them.

"Can we please avoid a firefight in the middle of the park?" Jones politely asked.

"What? You wanna take away all our fun?" Recker replied.

"I wouldn't dream of it."

When Recker and Haley got to the park, they spread out as they planned. Recker started walking to the vicinity of Judge Rocco's house, while Haley meandered through the park, looking for signs of anything that might look peculiar. As Recker walked along the street, he also kept his eyes peeled for any signs of trouble. Since he knew there might be someone already watching the Rocco house, Recker made sure he kept moving. He didn't want it to look like he was also watching the house in case he was spotted too.

Being alert as he usually was, Recker didn't see anything that looked suspicious. He walked around the block then stopped at the end of the street and leaned up against the side of a building. He was curious if Haley saw anything yet.

"Chris, you got anything on your end?"

"No. Not that I can see, anyway. I don't even know what I'm looking for, though."

"Well, you see the three guys we're looking for?"

"No. But I kind of doubt they're just gonna walk past me either," Haley said.

"Never know. Remember, they don't know we're here. So, they're not looking for us like we are for them."

"Yeah, I guess. Would be easier if we knew what they were gonna do."

"At least we have the time it's gonna go down," Recker said. "Other than that, we're just gonna have to wing it."

"You're right, it could be worse if we didn't know what time it was happening. Around the clock surveillance would be rough."

"Just keep your eyes peeled."

Recker looked at the time. It was twelve-thirty. A half hour until the nanny took the Rocco child for her afternoon walk in the stroller. Recker anxiously watched every person who walked by, every car that drove by, hoping he'd spot one of the men he was looking for. He didn't, though. At least not yet. Once one o'clock hit, he looked down at the Rocco house and noticed the front door swing open. He noticed the nanny coming out with the baby in her arms.

Recker let Haley know. "Chris, they're coming out of the house now."

"Roger that."

Recker got ready to move and started walking toward the park. He was walking slow enough that, eventually, the nanny and baby would walk past him. He thought it would look much more natural than if he tailed them the entire way there. He periodically stopped and looked at the scenery, pretending to take pictures of the nature around him to give them a chance to catch up to him.

"Anything yet on your end?" Haley asked.

"All clear so far."

Recker looked back to make sure he didn't see anyone else tailing the nanny. He didn't notice anything suspicious though. But it didn't mean they weren't there. He kept walking to the park then pretended he had a phone call. He stopped and made some hand gestures as he blurted some words out to keep up the ruse in case anyone was watching him. After a few more minutes, the nanny walked past him. Recker gave her a smile as she did, still pretending to be on the phone. He gave her a head start on him before he started walking behind her. The entire way to the park, Recker was waiting for the sound of screeching tires against the asphalt, or frantic screams of someone about to make the child heist, something chaotic that would indicate what was about to happen. A warning. But there was none. As they got to the park entry, Recker let his partner know where they were.

"We're making our way into the park now," Recker said. "Where you at?"

"I'm right smack in the middle."

"OK. We're coming in by 19th street. Come this way and then we'll switch off."

"On my way."

Recker followed the nanny into the park, keeping a safe distance between them. After a few minutes, he saw Haley walking in their direction. Once Recker saw him, he peeled off and took a different path. He still stayed in the area and kept an eye on their subject as Haley moved in closer. Once the nanny took a seat on one of the benches, Haley did the same, not too far from her position. After a few minutes, another young woman came along, also with a stroller. As far as Recker and Haley knew, she wasn't supposed to be meeting anyone. Recker quickly contacted Jones to see if he had an idea of what was going on.

"David, the nanny's meeting another woman," Recker said. "You know who it is?"

"Hold on, I'm checking."

Haley stealthily took a picture of the two women and sent it to Jones. "David, just sent you a picture of them."

Jones looked at his phone as soon as it alerted him of the message. He quickly looked at the photo as he started comparing it to people he had on his screen.

"Anything yet?" Recker asked, getting impatient.

"I'm still checking," Jones replied.

"Soon would be nice. I guess it's not necessary, though, it's not like we're trying to prevent a kidnapping or anything."

"Sarcasm will get you nowhere, Michael, and it won't help me get the information faster either."

"I know, I know."

Jones was typing away speedily, swiveling his chair between two computers. On one, he was comparing pictures of who he suspected the woman might be, as well as checking phone records on the other computer. He was trying to go as fast as he could, knowing what was at stake. Recker knew Jones was trying to get the information as quickly as possible and it wasn't so easy to get it within a few minutes.

"They're talking and laughing," Recker said. "I see a lot of smiles so maybe they already know each other."

As they waited for Jones to give them something, Recker's eyes scanned the area, though he still didn't see anything out of the ordinary. The park seemed like it was hustling with people and Recker just couldn't see how they were going to kidnap the child with all these people around. Of course, then he thought maybe that's what the kidnappers were counting on. Maybe they were going to use the crowd to blend in to disguise their movements. After five more minutes, Jones finally came up with something.

"I've got her," Jones said.

"Who is she?" Recker asked.

"Her name is Jordan. Her and the nanny are good friends it appears. Seems they meet at the park three or four days a week. I hacked into their text messages. They plan these outings in advance, agreeing to meet each other the night before or that morning."

"She have a criminal record? Maybe she's just setting her up."

"No. Seems as though they went to college

together. Nothing in her background would suggest she would be mixed up in something like this either."

"Are they both nannies?"

"No, the baby Jordan has is actually hers. It's an eight-month-old boy," Jones said.

"All right, thanks. We'll keep our eyes open."

Recker and Haley did just that for the next hour as the two women sat on the bench and talked with their babies in their strollers. The girls did get up and walk around for a bit, followed closely by Haley. Recker took an alternate path and tried to get out ahead of them. They walked around the park until two-thirty, eventually saying goodbye and going their separate ways. The nanny immediately started walking back to the Rocco house, with Recker and Haley still on her tail. They staggered their positions, so they weren't seen walking together.

The two Silencers were on high alert, expecting something to happen. It didn't happen in the park, so they figured it would happen on the way back. Every car that drove by, every person they passed, Recker was ready to pounce and unleash his fury on the kidnappers. They were slightly surprised that once the nanny got back to the house, nothing had happened. Since Recker walked by the house earlier, he didn't want to do it again and get made. This time, Haley walked past the home to see if he could make out something Recker couldn't. But just like his partner, Haley didn't find anything unusual either. After Haley walked around the block, he met back up with Recker near the park entrance to figure out their next move. Before they did anything, Recker let Jones know everything seemed clear.

"David, the nanny's back in the house with the baby. Nobody made a move toward them."

"Well, we did say that we did not know the date that this was supposed to happen," Jones replied. "Perhaps tomorrow will be the day."

"Yeah, maybe. We're gonna stay here for a little while and see if we spot anything."

"You don't think the kidnappers are there, do you?"

"I dunno. Probably not. But you never know. Maybe they were here watching too, trying to make sure their plan was good," Recker said.

Once Recker hung up, he and Haley walked back into the park, with a careful eye out on spotting any of the men they saw in the photos.

"You really think they might be here?" Haley asked.

Recker shrugged. "I don't know. Usually something like this needs precision planning, right?"

"Yeah."

"Well, you gotta go out and scout the location and predict any issues that might pop up. Can't do that behind a computer screen or in a dark, dingy room. Gotta go to the spot it's gonna go down and get your eyes on everything directly. If you were kidnapping somebody here, what would you do?"

"I'd probably spend a week or two in the spot it was

going to happen and observe everything, try to pick up on any patterns," Haley answered.

"Same as I would do."

"You don't think maybe we got spotted, do you? Maybe today was the day, and they made us, and it spooked them."

Recker made a face and shook his head, not sure he could really answer his question. "Tough to say. On one hand, I kind of hope that's the case. Maybe that would mean they change tactics and leave the child out of this."

"But it could also mean they do something completely different or out of left field," Haley said. "Something we don't see coming."

Recker sighed, readily acknowledging it as the truth. "I know."

They walked through the park for another hour, trying to find any of their potential suspects, or see if anything seemed odd to them. Still nothing seemed unusual. Then they walked along the perimeter of the park, observing buildings across the street to see if one of them could be used in the caper. They also looked for cars, specifically vans, or trucks that could be used for a getaway. Recker assumed the kidnappers would not use a car that could be easily identifiable and would choose an unmarked van so the inside couldn't be seen through a back window.

After they spent a considerable amount of time

walking around the area, they concluded there was nothing else they could do there. They weren't frustrated, but they were a little dismayed they didn't see or hear anything that would get them closer to figuring out the kidnapping plan. Though they didn't feel like they wasted their day, they sure didn't feel like it was productive either.

"Let's head back to the office and see if we can find something else out on this," Recker said, tapping Haley on the arm.

They went back to the office, hoping Jones had found something else, anything at all, that would help them. Recker would settle for the tiniest of details right then. When they walked in, Jones didn't bother to turn around and greet them. Instead, he was hard at work trying to come up with the little nugget they needed to get ahead of the situation.

"Please tell me you've come up with something," Recker said, walking past the desk on his way to the refrigerator. He grabbed two twenty-ounce soda bottles and tossed one of them over to Haley.

The look on Jones' face, along with his sigh and the shaking of his head, basically answered his question for him. Jones was trying to find that small kernel of information they could use, but it just wasn't happening. Nothing he did or tried provided anything more than they already knew.

"What about these guys' addresses?" Haley asked.

"Why don't we just find where they live and go take them out?"

"That would certainly be one way to do it if I was able to find out that piece of information," Jones replied.

"You can't locate them?" Recker asked, taking a sip of his soda.

"I cannot. Wherever they are, they are not using credit cards, so I can't tell if they're in a hotel or what."

"What about using their phones to get a trace?" Haley asked.

"I've tried. The signals bounce around several locations."

"So, they're either using some type of blocker or maybe they're moving around a lot," Recker said.

"What's even more disturbing is that I haven't gotten any trace on their phones since late last night."

"What's so disturbing about that?"

"I've gone through their phone records for the past month and they communicate with each other quite often. Daily. Now, just before they're supposed to do a big job, they've suddenly gone silent?"

Recker nodded, trying to wrap his head around it. "Usually it's the reverse. Usually you start talking more as the job gets closer, wanting to make sure all the details are accounted for, making sure there's no slip-ups."

"So maybe they're not as close to pulling the job as we thought they were," Haley said.

Jones threw his hands up, exasperated. "I just don't know. All indications from the conversations I saw and heard was that the job was going to be done soon."

"There's another possibility," Recker said.

"Which is?" Jones asked.

"That they switched phones."

Jones titled his head and raised his eyebrows, intrigued by the suggestion, realizing that he may have been on to something. "Yes, I guess that is possible."

"Most crews wouldn't go to that level, but some might. Especially those who are concerned about their communications being tapped or that they're being followed. They either switch to another line of communication or they might have just swapped phones entirely."

"If they did, then that would likely mean that the job is in fact imminent."

"Probably," Recker said. "Any way you can tell if they got new phones?"

The painful expression on Jones' face indicated that it would be unlikely. "I very seriously doubt it. If they're smart enough to know to switch phones, they're equally likely to be smart enough to know to get burner phones that they'll pay for with cash."

"And avoid cameras," Haley said.

"That too. It is also likely that as soon as the job is over that they would toss those new phones away somewhere."

"I guess the only thing we can do is keep showing up at the park and hope we nail them."

Recker sighed, knowing that was the only thing they could do. "Yep, that's about it. There's always tomorrow."

7

The rest of the threesome's day was spent working on the kidnapping case, trying to get any type of lead, since all they had for sure was the place and time. But at least it was better than nothing. They couldn't find any other information on the group than they already had. They had names, pictures, phone numbers, but they didn't have their current location. And their phones had been silent for much of the day except for two or three incoming phone calls from outside sources that went unanswered. They were coming up on seven o'clock and were close to calling it a day.

"We're pretty sure the Jordan girl isn't involved somehow?" Recker asked.

"I would stake my five-hundred-thousand-dollar pension on it," Jones remarked, getting an unusual stare from both Recker and Haley, knowing full well he didn't have any such pension.

"Always nice to bet with something you don't have."

Jones almost chuckled, but instead just gave a wry smile. "Indeed. No, but really, there's nothing that I can tell that she is even remotely involved."

"Check her phone records?" Haley asked.

"I have. Hasn't matched up to any of the kidnappers."

"You check into our police problem at all?" Recker said.

"I've dipped my toes into the water, so to speak."

"And?"

"It's still very early, but no promising leads to start with," Jones said. "But as I mentioned this morning, we don't have much to work with."

"Well, we know the type of bullet for all four shootings," Haley said. "That's something."

"Yes, it's something. But not much. From the reports I've seen, markings on the bullets indicate they were all fired from the same weapon. But connecting that to anybody right now is going to be tricky."

"We're gonna have to figure out how the four victims all knew each other. There has to be a connection between them," Recker said.

"We say victims, but in actuality, there were only three. Don't forget, the undercover officer did survive."

"Then the question will be, was he targeted specifically, or was he targeted because of something he was doing at that particular time and spot?"

"And we just simply do not have enough information to be able to tell right now," Jones replied.

"I hope somebody finds out something before another body drops."

"You keep saying that as if it's a forgone conclusion. You don't know that to be the case. It could be that perhaps those four were involved in something that we haven't yet discovered and that will be the end of it."

"You're thinking the cops were into something dirty?" Haley asked, assuming that was what Jones was referencing.

"I'm not thinking or saying anything of the kind. Perhaps it was something illegal, perhaps it was not. I don't know. And neither does anyone else. And it is way too soon to tell whether this is part of a larger scale plan that will end up with more victims or whether this was a more narrow-minded event."

"I like to prepare for the worst," Recker said.

"Yes, I know. And I'm not saying you won't be proven correct, eventually. I'm just saying right now, we don't have enough information to head in any specific direction."

"Well, hopefully there won't be anything else. But I have a feeling we won't be that lucky."

Recker stood, ready to call it a night. Jones and Haley were going to keep working, since they didn't have anyone at home waiting for them.

"Sure you guys don't mind me taking off?" Recker asked, feeling bad about leaving them.

"Not at all, Michael," Jones answered. "Not much else for you to do here, anyway. Go home, take care of your beautiful and better other half."

"I'll stay if you really want me to."

"We got it, Mike," Haley said. "No biggie."

"It always feels like I'm abandoning you guys when I leave before you do."

"Well, I never leave so that's a moot point for me," Jones replied.

"True."

"Yeah, and I don't have much else to do anyway," Haley said. "If I had a girlfriend, maybe I'd be joining you in walking out the door."

Jones shuffled his shoulders around like he got some chills. "I shudder at the thought."

"What? Don't want me to ever have one?"

Jones stopped typing and turned to look at him. "It's not that I don't wish you to ever have a woman, if that is what you desire. My only hope is that if that does become the case, that you don't engage in a five-year back-and-forth battle with yourself in whether you actually want one."

Recker squinted as he stared at Jones. "You're referring to me, aren't you?"

Jones threw his arms up. "I'm not mentioning any names. I'm just saying, to know what you want and not waffle back and forth for five years on the subject."

"Hey, it was not five years. You're exaggerating."

"Am I?" Jones asked. "OK, maybe the five years is a bit much of a reach. But you have to admit that your feelings for Mia sometimes changed with the weather."

"They did not. I always cared for Mia. I just wasn't sure if it was the best idea to get involved."

"Yes, I know, every other day."

Recker gave his friend a bit of a nasty face, though it was only in joking. He realized it took him longer than it probably should have to truly embrace the feelings he had for his now-girlfriend. Jones then turned back to Haley to continue the conversation.

"All I can say is, be glad that you weren't here to live through the torture of him sorting out his feelings," Jones said, continuing the tease. "It was almost like he was back in high school trying to figure out whether he should ask out a girl in his class for a date or something."

Recker couldn't help but let out a laugh at the reference. "It was not. Now you're being overly dramatic."

Haley also started laughing at the friendly banter between the two partners. "Well, I promise if it ever happens that I'll try not to act like I'm in high school again."

"All I ask is that if it does happen, make sure it's someone who's as reliable and trustworthy as Mia," Jones said. "God forbid you get involved with someone and break up with them after a month and then we get police knocking down the office door."

"Did you guys ever have any hesitancy about that with Mia? I mean, any doubt at all?"

Jones shook his head. "Not one. But she proved her worth and loyalty very early on before they even dated so it was not so much of an issue."

"I would trust her with anything," Recker said.

"Speaking of your beautiful girlfriend, I take it that she's home tonight?"

"Yeah, why?"

Jones shrugged. "No reason. Just asking. That's usually the only time you leave, when she's home."

"Is that a problem?"

"No, not at all. I told you, you've never shirked your duties here. You just proved it last night by meeting the detective after hours. So, go home, spend time with your girlfriend, and give her some extra kisses from me."

"Yeah, me too," Haley said.

"I'm sure that won't be too much of a problem. The extra kisses that is," Jones said with a smirk.

Recker feigned being mad and stormed toward the door. "I'm not sitting here and taking this ribbing from you guys."

Jones and Haley couldn't help but laugh. "We'll see you in the morning," Jones said.

"Assuming you're still able to stand up after...," Haley said.

"Not listening to it," Recker playfully said, closing the door behind him before Haley could finish the joke.

After Recker left, Jones and Haley continued with their work.

"You don't have to stay here, you know," Jones said. "You can take the rest of the night if you want."

"Eh, it's like I told Mike, I don't really have much else to do, anyway."

"As you prefer."

"Besides, I still feel like I have more to learn. I'm a few years behind you guys at deciphering all this stuff," Haley said. "I think the more time I spend in here, the better off I'll be."

"I wouldn't think too much about that. You've done a very good job at assimilating into everything these past few months."

"You or Mike haven't had any regrets about bringing me in or anything, have you?"

Jones stopped working and looked at him. "Not for a second. Why, do you get that impression?"

Haley shook his head. "No, not at all. I just wanted to make sure I've been doing all right and that I haven't made any stupid mistakes."

"No need to fret about that. You're exactly what Mike and I were hoping for. We couldn't have asked for or expected to get a better candidate than you."

"Good."

Jones continued looking at him, trying to analyze

Haley's face, hoping there wasn't more to it than what they just said. "You're not feeling dissatisfied, are you? Or regret coming aboard?"

Haley put his hand up and smiled, trying hard to reassure his boss it wasn't the case. "No, really. I love being here. I like being around you guys. I like doing the work. It's a lot better than what I was doing before. So, no, everything's fine, really."

"OK. I was starting to think maybe you were looking to get out or resign or something," Jones said.

Haley shook his head. "Wouldn't dream of it. That's why I was asking if you guys were pleased with me so far. I just... I really like and enjoy being here and being part of the team."

After they finished their little exchange, they kept working straight up until nine. It didn't seem like it did much good, though, as they didn't find out anything new about the Rocco case. It was at that point Jones felt the need to call it a night as well and told Haley to go home and rest up.

"Well, there's not much else we can do tonight," Jones said. "Hopefully tomorrow is a more fruitful day for us."

"You think it'll go down tomorrow?"

"One thing's for sure, it's going to be soon."

"We'll be ready," Haley said.

After eating dinner with Mia, they both tried to relax on the couch for a while and watched TV. Mia had previously asked what case they were working on, so she was already aware of the situation with the judge. As they were watching a movie, she suddenly sat up, Recker's arm sliding from her shoulders. Mia turned to face him with a look on her face like she was about to surprise him with something.

"I've got it," she said.

Recker looked at her curiously, not sure what she was referring to. "You've got what?"

"Your problem."

Recker let out a laugh. "Which one? I've got several."

"Your judge problem. You know, with the baby."

"What about it?"

"You said you guys couldn't figure out how they were going to take the baby in the middle of a big park with a lot of people around."

"Yeah?"

"Well, I figured it out," Mia said.

"You have?"

"Don't you see? It's so obvious."

Recker wasn't sure if she really had a satisfactory answer or not, but wasn't going to dismiss it yet either. "Well then, please tell."

"They would have to create some type of diversion," Mia said, getting up from the couch. She started walking around the room, getting into the moment like she was an old-time movie detective as she thought about the crime.

But Recker wasn't impressed just yet. "We've already figured that part."

Mia stopped and pointed her finger at him. "Yes, but how are they going to do it?"

"Uh, we still don't know yet."

A huge smile came over Mia's face as she started to relay her thoughts. "They'll have to need the help of a woman."

Recker immediately knocked the idea. "There's no woman in the group. It's a three-man team."

"That you know of. Listen, they'll need the help of a woman to pull this off."

"And just how do you figure that?"

"They'll obviously need to get up close to get her, right?" Mia asked.

"Yeah."

"If I'm out walking a baby, and a strange man, or men, coming walking up to me, I'm gonna feel a little taken aback. The threat level's gonna go up a little. Even if they look completely nice and normal."

"It's not normal for men to gawk at other peoples' babies," Recker said, catching her point.

"Right. But if a woman does that, it's not so unnatural. I wouldn't necessarily think twice if another woman came up to me and did it."

Recker lifted his head up and looked at the ceiling as he thought about what she was saying. It certainly made sense, but it didn't really give them much else to work with.

"I mean, I can go along with all that, but it doesn't get us any closer," Recker said. "There's no woman that we know of on the crew. It's possible they could bring someone in, or have someone that they know, but we still don't know who that would be. Doesn't really tell us how either. I'm sure, even if it's a woman, they're not just gonna walk up to the nanny, snatch the baby out of the stroller, and run out of the park."

"Probably not."

"As soon as the nanny realizes the baby's been taken, she's gonna start screaming her head off and alert everyone in the area. There's no guarantee that woman's gonna make it out of the park at that point."

A confident look came over Mia's face, thinking she came up with the answer. "But not if she doesn't know the baby has been taken."

"Well, yeah, that's the issue. How are they gonna do that?"

"It's simple."

"How's that?" Recker asked.

"They won't wait until they get too deep into the park. It'll be right when she goes in, or right when she leaves."

"And just what are they gonna do?"

"The old switcheroo," Mia answered.

"The what?"

"They'll switch babies."

"And just how do you think they're going to do that?" Recker asked.

"I've got it. I've got it."

"OK?"

"Right when she enters the park, there'll be a woman," Mia said, then slapped her hands together as she changed course. "No, make that a man and a woman."

"Why?"

"For a diversion. I bet they'll pretend to be a couple, and they'll approach her as she walks into the park. Maybe they'll pretend to bump into her or maybe they'll just start talking about the baby or something."

Though it was beginning to make some amount of sense to Recker, he still wasn't convinced that would be the actual plan. "And how will they take the child?"

"While the woman is conversing with the nanny, the guy will take off with the baby."

"And she'll just be OK with him taking off with the kid?"

"Of course not. They'll do something to distract her," Mia answered.

"Oh, of course," Recker said in a mocking manner.

Mia paced around the room for another minute as she continued to think of the plot. She then got another look on her face like she just figured something out, then walked over to the couch and stood in front of her boyfriend as she explained.

"What if they have the same exact stroller?" she asked.

"Did they get a buy one, get one free deal?" Recker sarcastically said.

Not amused, Mia rolled her eyes. "Don't be silly. You said there's probably a good chance they've been staking her out, right?"

"Yeah."

"Then they probably took pictures of her with the stroller, then bought the same one."

Recker raised his eyebrows, curled his lip, and tilted his head, thinking maybe she was onto something. "Possible."

"I will bet you anything that's how it's gonna go down."

"Anything, huh?"

"Well, almost anything," she seductively said. "What? You think I'm wrong or I'm completely out of my mind?"

"No, I can't deny it makes some sense."

"I'll bet that the nanny enters the park, and another couple walks over to her and starts talking. They'll have the same stroller. The woman will distract her somehow, then the man will switch strollers and quickly head back out of the park while the women are still talking. The nanny won't even know what's going on until it's too late."

"Which means it's likely they'd have a getaway car nearby," Recker said.

"So? Did I solve your problem for you?" Mia happily asked, holding her arms out wide.

"Well, I guess you will have if that's actually how it happens."

"Think about it."

"Uh, I am."

"No, I mean, there's a three-man crew you said, right?"

"Yeah."

"So, there's one man waiting in the car, one man in the park with the stroller who's the getaway man or whatever you call him, and the third guy is milling around, ready to run interference if needed," Mia explained.

Recker folded his arms and put his left hand over his mouth as he looked at his girlfriend and thought about her idea. He couldn't readily discount it as he believed it was a credible and thought out plan. Whether it was what the kidnappers would do was another story. But it was something to think about. They talked about it for a few more minutes and Recker thought he should call Jones and see what he thought of the plan. Just before he did, though, Mia stopped him, having a few more ideas to run past him.

"You know what else I was thinking?" she asked.

Recker couldn't believe she had more to add. "What, did you just watch the mystery movie of the week or something?"

Mia waved her hand at him. "Oh, stop. You know, I'm off tomorrow."

Recker didn't pick up on the hint. "Yeah? I know you are."

"So. I was thinking, maybe I could go with you and help."

Recker immediately put his hands up to stop her from going any further. "No, no, no, no, no. Absolutely not."

"Why not? I can help."

"Didn't we decide a long time ago that you weren't going to do that type of stuff anymore?" Recker asked. "You remember what happened when you tried to do that?"

"You always bring that up."

"To make sure you remember it."

"I didn't know what I was doing then," Mia said.

"And you do now?"

"It's not like I'd be going out on my own. You'd be there, Chris would be there, I'd only be going to help."

Recker shook his head several times. "No. Not gonna happen."

"Don't be stubborn. You could use the help."

"I've got help."

"Mike, why won't you let me help you?"

"One, because it's not necessary. Two, because you're not trained for it," Recker answered. "Why are you so interested in it, anyway?"

Mia shrugged, not wanting her reasons to sound stupid. "I just want to be important to you."

Recker quickly stood and put his arms around her.

"Of course you're important to me. Why would you even say that?"

"I dunno."

"Listen, you've done more for me than you even know, or that I could ever say. You're the most important thing in my life."

She put her head on his chest. "I know. I just... I wanna feel like I can help you."

"You know you've helped me. In more ways than I can count."

They sat back down on the couch as they continued their conversation.

"But if I'm right, then you might need another person," Mia said.

"And how do you figure that?"

"There'd be three people there. The two guys, plus the girl, not even counting the driver. Now, what if you and Chris get caught up in a fight with the two guys and the woman decides to take things into her own hands and grabs the baby herself?"

"That's a lot of if's and maybe's, don't you think?" Recker asked. "I mean, you're acting like all this is guaranteed to happen. This isn't like a definite, you know."

"But what if it does?"

"Why are you so hell-bent on coming along? You've never been like this before."

Mia shrugged. "I don't know. Maybe it's because I'm off tomorrow and have nothing else to do. Maybe it's because I just want to spend more time with you. I don't know. Why are you so against it?"

"Because I don't want you to get hurt."

"You and Chris will be there. What's the worst that could happen to me?"

"Uh, you want me to go down the list? How about if we get in their way and they come up shooting? Ever think of that?"

Mia rolled her eyes, knowing he had a point, though she didn't want to acknowledge it. "How about if I ask David?"

"You're gonna ask David?"

"Why not? If he's OK with it, would you agree?"

"No!"

"Why not?" Mia asked.

"Because he's not your boyfriend, and he's not the one who'd be out there with you."

"You are a stubborn man; do you know that?"

"So I've been told."

Recker then walked into the kitchen and called Jones to see what he thought of Mia's idea.

"And I wanna talk to him before you hang up," Mia said. "And don't tell him to say no before you hand me the phone."

Recker rolled his eyes and sighed, but agreed anyway. As soon as Jones answered, Recker started to tell him Mia's plan in detail, remembering everything she said without leaving a single thing out.

"So, what do you think?" Recker asked.

"I would say that it certainly seems plausible."

"What about a woman? Can you filter out who that might be?"

"Well I've already compiled a list of known associates," Jones said.

"Are there any women on it?"

"Yes, there are several."

"Any way to narrow it down?"

"I guess I could work on it a little bit for the rest of the night. I can't say I will definitely be able to pinpoint one woman, though. But I'll see what I can do."

"So, you think it could go down that way?" Recker asked.

"I definitely do. I could see that scenario happening. I can also say that I can envision just about any other scenario happening as well, considering we don't have any leads on how it's going to go down."

"All right, I guess we can talk about it more in the morning."

Mia cleared her throat, making sure Recker heard her before he hung up. He looked over at her, and though he didn't really want to hand the phone over, did so anyway.

"David?" Mia said.

"Hello."

"Mike didn't mention it to you, but what would you think about me going out with them tomorrow?"

Jones was silent for a while, not sure how to respond. He was almost positive it was a trick question.

"David?"

"Oh, I'm... honestly not sure what to say."

"Well, would you have a problem with me going out with Mike and Chris to help out?"

Jones hesitated again, though for not quite as long. "And what did Mike say?" he asked, finding it hard to believe that Recker would have approved it.

"Well he said no. But I think I can help and I think I can be useful."

"I'm going to go along with him."

"But why?"

"Because I'm not getting in the middle of any of your spats," Jones said.

"We're not having a spat."

"Why are you getting me in the middle of this?"

"Aren't you technically in charge?" Mia asked.

"Well..."

"David, if there turns out to be a woman there, don't you think I could help if Mike and Chris are busy?"

"Umm, possibly. Didn't you swear off doing this type of stuff a long time ago?"

"Why does everyone keep saying that? I can handle it. Besides, it's not like I'd be by myself. Mike and Chris will be there."

Jones didn't want to get into an argument, or a long drawn out conversation about the subject, and just hoped to end the discussion as quickly as possible.

"Well, let me think on it for the night and I'll talk to Mike about it in the morning."

"You're just trying to get rid of me."

"I would never."

"Yeah right. You have no intention of saying yes or going against Mike."

"I have gone against Mike many times," Jones said.

"Yeah, but not when it comes to me."

"Well there are boundaries."

Mia sighed, resigning herself to the fact that nobody was going to say yes to her proposal. "Fine. I know when I'm not wanted."

"Mia, it's not that. We just want to keep you safe."

"I know, I know. I know the line. Well would you mind if I at least came into the office tomorrow? At least let me do something."

"Are you off tomorrow?"

"Yes."

"I don't see the harm in that if Mike is willing."

"I'll probably have to beg, crawl, and pray for him to approve."

8

The team was all set up in their respective positions. Recker was down the street from the Rocco house, waiting for the nanny to step outside with the baby. Haley was wandering through the park, looking for a sign of potential trouble. He was particularly keeping an eye out for a man and a woman with the same kind of stroller the Rocco baby had. He'd been walking around for a half hour without any luck. Jones was in the office, still typing away, hoping to find some last-minute solution that would let the secret out of the bag. As they were waiting for the action to begin, Jones couldn't resist a last-minute shot across Recker's bow.

"Mike, how is the third wheel doing?" Jones asked.

Recker gritted his teeth as he thought of a reply. "Just fine."

"Hey, I object to being called a third wheel!" Mia

said.

Jones chuckled. "Sorry, it wasn't intended as an insult toward you."

"Uh, huh."

"Hey, you're the one that let her come along," Recker said.

"Don't lay this at my feet. She's your girlfriend," Jones replied.

"Are you guys seriously gonna do this?" Mia asked. "You're gonna argue about me knowing full well I can hear you?"

Recker let out a sigh that was clearly audible in everyone's earpiece.

"Something upsetting you, Mike?" Jones asked.

"No. Nothing at all."

"Don't get upset, Mike, you know I can be helpful here," Mia said.

Recker still wasn't that pleased that she was there. "How'd I let you talk me into this?"

"Because deep down you knew I was right."

"No, I don't think that was it. I think you did some trickery on me or something."

"Don't be ridiculous. I merely pointed out the facts, which were accurate, and you came around to my line of thinking, as you should have."

"I must've been out of my mind."

"Oh stop. I'll be fine. This will work."

"It working isn't what I'm worried about," Recker said.

"Mike, cool your jets."

Haley, who'd been carefully listening to the playful exchange, couldn't hold back any longer and let out an audible laugh.

"At least you're amusing to somebody," Jones said.

"You planned this all along, didn't you?" Recker asked.

"Planned what?" Mia sweetly replied, acting like she didn't know what he was talking about.

"Don't pretend like you're oblivious. You know darn well what I'm talking about."

Though Mia really did know, she wasn't going to give in. "I really don't know."

"You played it off like you wanted to go to the office this morning and help out with logistics and stuff. But you were really planning this all along, weren't you?"

Mia replied, trying to talk and sound as sweet and innocent as possible. "Honestly, Mike, I just wanted to help in the office. That's all."

Recker scoffed, letting out a laugh, knowing full well he was right. "That cute and innocent act isn't gonna work with me. You know I know."

"Excuse me, but did we just stumble into an old Abbott and Costello routine or something?" Jones asked.

"Maybe I should be glad I'm single," Haley said.

"Indeed."

"Really, Mike, if you didn't want me here then you should've just said so," Mia said.

"I did. Several times."

"Well, obviously you weren't persistent enough."

"Or some people are just hard headed and stubborn," Recker replied.

"Mike, don't self-deprecate yourself like that over the air in public."

Jones and Haley both laughed at the same time.

"Mike, you seem to have met your match," Jones said.

Recker opened his mouth to reply, but honestly couldn't come up with a reply and just waved his hand in the air a couple of times before letting it settle on his face. He shook his head and rubbed the sides of both temples and let his hand slide down his face and onto his neck as he looked up at the sky.

"What, nothing else to add?" Mia asked.

"Nope. Nothing."

As much as the team, maybe except Recker, seemed to be enjoying the playful banter amongst the couple, Jones looked at the time and knew they had to get down to business. It was only a few minutes before the nanny was due to leave the house.

"OK. It looks like playtime is over," Jones said. "We've only got five minutes to go on the countdown. Is everyone in place?"

Recker, Haley, and Mia all confirmed they were. They stationed Mia on a bench inside the park, near the entrance the nanny usually came in at. They figured if something did go down there, like she thought it might, she'd be right on top of it. And if it didn't, she could easily follow the nanny through the park without attracting anyone's suspicions. Mia fought hard to get to that point. She spent the entire night before trying to wear down Recker to let her come along. She talked the entire morning, first to Recker, then to Jones and Haley, about letting her tag with the group. Her and Recker got to the office a little after eight, and almost immediately, Mia started working on the team in the effort to let her get in on the park detail. After over three hours of her constant badgering, she finally got the blessing of Haley first. Once the first domino fell, she got Jones to see the light. Her boyfriend was the toughest case, as she knew it would be, and with the other two giving her the green light, Recker finally got worn down to the point where he saw the benefit in her joining the plan in the field. At least until she was out there. Once she was in place, Recker doubted why he let himself get talked into it. But Mia always was a special case with him. She had the ability to change his mind or persuade him to do something he really didn't want to like nobody else could.

Within a few minutes, the nanny came out of the house right on time. Recker was at his spot at the end of the street waiting for her. Just as he had the day before, he walked around the block to see if he noticed anyone else waiting for her. But just like before, he noticed nothing unusual.

"She's on the move," Recker said.

"Let's hope today's the day and we nip this thing in the bud," Jones replied.

Recker walked away from the park and down the street as the nanny walked closer, just to avoid the possibility of being spotted. Once she got near the intersection of 19th and Rittenhouse, Recker made a sharp turn and quickly walked back toward her, in anticipation of something happening soon.

"Hey, I just saw a man and a woman with the same type of stroller," Haley reported.

"Where at?" Recker replied.

"Uh, should be walking to you now."

"It's going down like Mia said."

"I'm on them."

"Mia, get ready," Jones said.

"I don't see anyone yet," she replied.

"You will. Just sit tight for now."

"We're entering the park," Recker said, walking briskly. "I'm only a few feet behind her."

"Mike, give her some space and just stand by the exit path for now," Jones said.

Recker complied with Jones' wishes and stood by the small iron gate and tried to look inconspicuous. There were several benches up ahead and a couple of paths leading away from his direction, but nothing was blocking his way so he couldn't catch up to them if they went in another direction. Plus, he figured Haley might get to them before he did, anyway. Recker continued looking around, hoping to see the couple his partner described. After a few minutes, he did.

"I see them," Recker said. "The nanny just sat down on a bench across from Mia."

"What do I do?" Mia asked.

"Nothing yet. Just relax. You only need to focus on the woman. Don't worry about anything else."

After five more minutes elapsed, the couple Haley reported were now within view. They were walking toward the nanny's position.

"I think we're about to get action," Recker said, looking around for other members of the crew.

"The guy is definitely one of them. Spot on image from his picture," Haley replied.

"I don't see the other two anywhere."

"I'm sure they're nearby," Jones said. "Stay alert."

Recker and Haley watched intently as the couple approached the nanny. They seemed friendly enough, striking up a conversation with her. They watched the three of them laughing about something, and the two women seemed to be getting along very well, almost looking like old friends. Recker's eyes then were diverted to another couple who were walking toward the same bench as the others.

"I don't believe it," he said with a whisper.

"What?" Jones asked.

"There's another couple with the same stroller."

"You're kidding."

"I wish I was."

"I see it," Haley said. "I recognize the guy. Same crew again."

The third couple arrived near the same bench as the others and also struck up a conversation with the group. After a minute, they were all talking, smiling, and laughing. Recker was as sure as ever they were going to pull a switch any minute, as soon as they found the right moment.

"Be on your toes," Recker said, getting ready to pounce.

A few more minutes went by and Recker observed one of the men getting ready to leave. One of the women was distracting the nanny, and the man switched strollers, taking the one with the Rocco baby in it. He bid the others goodbye and started walking away from the group as the rest of them continued chatting away. With the nanny being distracted by the women, and not looking at the strollers at that moment, she didn't have any clue the baby she was in charge of was being taken away.

"They just did it," Recker said. "They just pulled the switch."

"I saw it," Haley replied.

"Mia, you go toward the stroller for the baby."

"What about the woman?" Mia asked.

"Forget the woman. I'm going after that guy. If I take him out, I wanna make sure nobody else is around to snatch the kid while I'm busy."

"OK."

Mia did as Recker wanted and got up from her seat and started following the man who just left with the wrong stroller. Recker started running toward the man to cut him off from escaping. As he did, Haley moved into position between the group and the path the man just walked down. That way, if anyone saw Recker interfering, Haley would be ready to block them, giving his partner enough time to subdue the man and take control of the situation.

The plan seemed to work perfectly. Mia was right behind the man, ready to take control of the stroller once he lost his grip of it. She looked at Recker coming out of the corner of her eye. Recker ran across a patch of grass and past a couple of trees as he ran full force at the unsuspecting man. Wanting to catch him off-guard, Recker jumped at him as soon as he was within range. Recker gave him a flying cross body tackle, knocking them both to the ground. As soon as they wrestled on the concrete, Mia grabbed the stroller to make sure it didn't roll away, or fall into the wrong hands.

Recker had quickly straddled the man on the ground and gave him several punches to the face. The man was so stunned at what happened he didn't have much of a chance to fight back. As people started to look at the commotion, one of the other men ran toward them. Haley quickly put a stop to that though, spearing the man in the gut with his shoulder, knocking them onto the ground as well. Much like his partner, Haley also began delivering shots to the man's face.

The two women who had accompanied the crew members looked on in horror, realizing the plan was falling apart. Seeing the two men seemed to be subdued, the women quickly scurried out of the area. The nanny looked at them strangely and wasn't sure what was going on, wondering why they just ran off and left their babies and strollers behind. She looked in what she thought was her stroller and was horrified to discover it wasn't hers at all. Inside was only a child's doll. Quickly being taken over by panic, she reached into the other stroller and discovered there was only a doll inside that one as well. She backed up, a look of pure fear taking over her face. She then looked over and saw Mia standing there with what she hoped was her stroller and ran over to her. Mia saw her running over to her and smiled. She put her hand out to try to get the woman to calm down.

"It's OK," Mia said. "She's fine. She's fine."

"Oh my God, I can't believe this," the nanny said, picking the baby up out of the stroller. She held her tightly in her arms and hugged the child, thankful she was all right.

Mia rubbed the woman's back for a second and patted her on the shoulders to calm her down. "It's all over."

"Thank you so much. I don't even... I mean... what... what were they trying to do?"

"It was an..."

Before Mia could say too much, and more than she should have, Recker and Haley interrupted her. In anticipation of running into trouble, and trying to abide by Jones' wishes that they didn't use their guns, they brought zip ties with them to bind the suspect's hands together. Once they did that, Recker and Haley dragged their victims over to one of the benches and tied them to the bench until a police officer arrived and took them into custody. Once they approached the two women, a car hastily pulled out of a nearby parking spot and sped off. Recker could only assume it might have been the getaway car.

"Thanks for your help in watching the stroller, ma'am," Recker said, putting his hand out to shake Mia's hand, pretending as if he didn't know her.

Mia quickly picked up on the charade and shook his hand. "Oh, yes, no problem. Just glad I could help."

"I was just telling her, I don't know what happened," the nanny said. "I mean, what were they doing? Were they trying to take the baby?"

Recker nodded. "Unfortunately, they were. The two men are part of a criminal gang."

"But why did they come after us?"

"The baby is the daughter of a judge, correct?"

"Yeah. Were they trying to get back at her for something? Were they gonna hurt the baby?"

"We don't think so. We think it was part of a plan about an upcoming trial the judge has."

Recker was getting antsy still standing in the area and realized they had probably been there too long already and looked around for a police car.

"Well, we're gonna have to go. Just stay here until the police arrive and tell them what happened so these guys get put away," Recker said.

The nanny looked confused as she thought the two men standing in front of her were police. "Wait, you're not the police?"

Haley shook his head. "No, we're not."

"I just thought you were like undercover or detectives or something."

"Nope."

"Then how do you know all this?"

"That's not important. What is important is that the judge takes the necessary steps in protecting you and the baby. At least for the next couple of months," Recker said. "Police should be here soon, so you shouldn't have to wait long."

The nanny rubbed her head, feeling a little overwhelmed with it all. Recker noticed she wasn't looking so good.

"Perhaps this nice lady here would be willing to wait with you until the cops get here," Recker said.

"Yeah, I could do that," Mia replied.

"You guys can't stick around?" the nanny asked.

"No, I'm afraid not. Cops aren't exactly pleased with us either."

"What do I tell them about you?"

"Just tell them exactly what went down. If they ask who we were, just tell them The Silencer was here."

The nanny's eyes opened wide, almost in shock with what she just heard. "The Silencer? You're him?"

"In the flesh."

"I've heard so much about you."

Recker smiled. "Yeah. Well, I gotta go. You take care."

Recker and Haley then quickly walked away. As they left the park and crossed the street, they saw two police cars rolling into the area. As they walked away, he wanted to let his girlfriend know what they were doing.

"We'll be waiting in a restaurant over on Locust," Recker said. "Soon as you're done, walk over there."

"OK," Mia replied.

Recker then let Jones know the mission was over. "David, everything's done here."

"Excellent. Everything went off without issue then?" Jones asked.

"Well, all things considering. The two guys are apprehended, police should be taking them in soon. The nanny and baby are fine. The two women that were helping them got away. Not much we could do about that, though."

"They were the least that we should be concerned about. Like you said, all things considered, it was a good day's work."

"There was a car that I saw peel off after everything

went down. Might've been the third guy," Recker said. "Looked like a black SUV. Couldn't make anything out."

"I'll check nearby cameras and see if I can get a make on anything."

Recker hung up and continued walking toward Locust Street to wait until Mia finished up with the police.

"Mia should be alright back there, right?" Haley asked.

"Yeah, why?"

"I dunno. With the police and all."

"They don't know she's with us. I figured it might look more suspicious if she left with us. I didn't want anybody to connect her with me. It's better if it's thought she was just a passerby and happened to be in the area."

"Speaking of connecting people to you, you sure it was a wise idea to let that woman know who you were?" Haley asked.

Recker shrugged. "I don't know if it really matters at this point. Everyone knows who I am."

"She didn't until you told her."

"If they ask questions and show her a few pictures, she'll recognize it's me, anyway. Besides, I figure it's better if I identify myself to the public, let them know I'm there to help them, put a face to the name and the stories they've heard of me. That way, if they ever see me and recognize me, they'll know I'm there to help and won't call the police."

"I guess that makes sense. Kind of like preventive medicine."

"In any case, of all the people I've helped over the years I've been here, none of them have said a bad word to the police about me, or tried to give me up or something. Even ones who were just bystanders, or witnessed me doing something. I think the public knows I'm here to help them and accept it."

"Wish the police felt the same way," Haley said.

"Well, they gotta do what they gotta do. We both know that."

"Speaking of which, I guess we got some time to work on their problem now."

"Maybe, maybe not."

"Why not?"

"Well, this was a three-man crew, right?" Recker asked.

"Yeah."

"Well we only got two of them. And we don't know who those two women were with them. Are they part of their gang now, or were they just two girls they plucked off the street and promised a lot of money to if they helped them?"

"True."

"One thing's for sure, if one of these guys are still out there, this might not be over."

9

Three days had passed since the incident at the park. Recker and Haley had successfully stopped several other criminal acts since then. They had just finished an assignment and got back to the office after lunchtime. They brought back a sandwich for Jones, and after he finished it, they got down to work again. Jones informed them of an impending situation that was all too familiar to them. As Recker and Haley sat, Jones swiveled his chair around to talk about it.

"It looks as if we've got another problem with Judge Rocco."

"They going after the baby again?" Recker asked.

"Not at all. Now it seems as though they're going to go after the judge directly."

Recker looked confused. "You mean they're gonna try to kill her? What sense would that make?"

Haley agreed with the assessment. "Yeah, even if they kill this judge, another one will still be assigned. It's not like they can just kill every judge they come across."

"It's not quite that dire," Jones said. "I don't believe they plan on killing her. They know that would be a stupid move. I do believe, though, that they plan on making decisions, and life in general, very rough for her."

"In what way?" Recker asked.

"I believe they're going to try to scare and intimidate her."

"How are they going to do that?"

"That I'm not yet sure."

"What'd you pick up on?"

"Text message from the last remaining member of the gang," Jones answered.

"I thought that was silent for the last few days?"

"It was. Until this morning. I picked up on a message between him and another number which I have not yet identified."

"Get a location at least?" Recker said.

"Yes. It's not much help, however. Whoever is on the other end of the line, they're not in this city."

"Where are they?"

"I've got it narrowed down to a location in Boston."

"Boston?"

"I can only assume it's either a superior or possibly whoever hired him," Jones said.

"What did the message say?" Haley asked.

"It was from Ross asking how they wanted him to get to her."

"Vague wording," Recker replied. "Could be just about anything."

"They indicate a time frame?" Haley asked.

Jones shook his head. "No."

"Gonna be the same deal again. We're gonna have to stake out her house again."

"Maybe," Recker said.

Just as the threesome was about to delve into things further, Recker's phone rang. It was Malloy. Curious as to what he wanted, Recker quickly answered.

"Hey."

"Just wanted to pass something along to you," Malloy said.

"OK?"

"Our mutual friend wanted to have another conversation with you."

"Our mutual friend? Are we talking about the one who has a shiny badge and lots of cool little gadgets at their disposal?" Recker asked, trying to make light of it.

"That's the one."

"It's not necessary. I'll call him directly."

"Fine with me. I'm just passing it along. By the way, how you doing on that?"

"Who's asking? You or Vincent?"

"Uh, I guess you could say both," Malloy answered.

"I didn't know you cared so much about police problems."

"I don't. Just a passing interest."

"Well just so you know, and you can tell Vincent, that we haven't made much progress on it yet."

"Shame."

"Yeah, I can tell you're heartbroken," Recker said.

As soon as Recker hung up, he let the others know what the conversation was about. "I'm already tired of going through third parties for this."

"Why not just give Andrews a phone number to reach us?" Haley asked.

Recker gave Jones a look to see if he agreed with the idea. While Recker was fine with it, he knew Jones was a little apprehensive about mingling with the police department.

"What do you think?" Recker asked.

"I suppose it can do no real harm," Jones said, opening one of the drawers, revealing a bunch of prepaid phones. "None of them can be traced back to us."

"Which one?"

"Take your pick. As I said, it doesn't matter."

"And when this is over, if he decides to be a big man and take us on, you're sure none of these can come back to here?"

"No, they've all been reprogrammed to bounce off towers far away from here," Jones replied.

Recker picked up one of the phones then closed

the drawer. As he deliberated calling the detective, he wondered what else the officer wanted. They hadn't heard of any other incidents going down. Maybe he was just wondering if Recker made any progress. After a few more minutes, Jones found Andrews' phone number and wrote it down on the desk. Recker then wasted no more time in calling. The detective picked up after the second ring.

"This is Detective Andrews."

"I hear you wanted to meet," Recker said.

Andrews had just gotten into his car and was about to head back to his office, but put his car back in park as he took the phone call. He looked out both front windows as well as the rear-view mirror to make sure no one was around listening, not that they really could with the windows up and the air conditioning on. But he was a little paranoid about someone overhearing him talking to the wanted man.

"Uh, yeah, yeah, I did," Andrews said.

"I'm a little busy right now, can't really get away. Talking on here will have to suffice."

"No, that's fine. I've heard about how busy you are."

"You have?" Recker asked, not knowing what he was referring to.

"Yeah. Heard about that stuff that went down at Rittenhouse Park the other day."

"How you know that was me?"

"Oh, uh, the girl identified you. Said you told her who you were."

"Oh."

"Yeah. Good stuff. Believe it or not, you have more friends in the department than you might think," Andrews said.

Recker was sure he wasn't calling just to talk about his exploits and quickly shifted the conversation around. "So, what else is up?"

"Oh, yeah, I was just wondering if you'd come up with anything on our little problem?"

"Not yet. We don't really have a whole lot to go on," Recker said.

"Yeah, I know. Well, we might have a little more now."

"Why's that?"

"We've got another body," Andrews answered.

"Damn."

"It's actually the first cop that got shot. That under-cover officer I told you about. Shot dead walking out of his house this morning."

As he was speaking, Recker put his hand over the phone and snapped his fingers at Jones with his other hand to get his attention. As Recker put the phone back to his ear, he made a circling motion to Jones to let him know something was going on.

"Killed this morning?" Recker asked, loud enough for Jones to hear.

Taking his cue, Jones immediately started typing away to pull up whatever snippets of information he could find. It wasn't long before he found a few online articles from some of the local newspaper and television websites.

"I guess it's the same shooter?" Recker asked.

"Well, we can't definitely say for sure right now. The bullet's still inside him and there was no other evidence at the scene. From the size of the hole in his chest, it looked pretty close to the same as what we've been dealing with."

"He was definitely targeted then."

"I know."

"There's gotta be a common link between the two cops and that dealer," Recker said. "The other guy probably happened like you said, saw something he wasn't supposed to."

"As far as we can tell, there's no links between the two officers. They're from different districts."

"I'm sure you've gone deep into their packets, is there any chance they're dirty or involved in something?"

Sometimes officers took offense when someone mentioned one of them being dirty, but Andrews didn't even give it a second thought. He quickly responded. "I dunno. Everyone we've talked to, friends, partners, relatives, other cops, nobody's said a bad word about them."

"That doesn't mean they weren't into something," Recker said.

"I know. But from what we can gather, they were just hardworking cops. Nothing more. Now, if you were to ask me to put money on the line and say that, I wouldn't do it. But we haven't uncovered anything that would lead us in that direction."

"What about former partners? Other districts they've worked in? Any commonalities there?"

Once again, Andrews rebuffed the point. "No. Neither one of them have ever worked in the same district at any point in time."

"Ever investigated the same people?" Recker asked.

"Nope. We've checked. I mean, if you think it'll help, I can give you copies of their records."

"It's not necessary. I can get them on my own."

"You can? How?" Andrews asked.

"Not important. What is important is if you've identified any other officers that you think may be in danger? Any partners, former partners, other cops they've been in contact with, anything like that?"

"No. Another dead end."

"You don't have a whole lot going for you right now, do you?"

"Now you see why I reached out to you when I did," Andrews answered.

"All right, well, we'll dig into their files further and see if we can find some common links."

"Thanks. I appreciate that."

"In the meantime, take this number down," Recker said, giving the detective the number to the prepaid phone. "If you need anything else, get in touch with me there. I don't like going through Vincent for things."

"Yeah, no problem."

"Just a warning, if you try to trace it, it's gonna lead you nowhere, so save yourself a lot of time and aggravation by not even bothering."

"I figured as much. Didn't think you'd give me anything that would lead straight to you," Andrews said. "Not that it would matter. Remember, I'm one of the cops that thinks you're doing good for this city."

"Well, feelings sometimes have a habit of changing. I just wanted to let you know in advance."

"Understood."

"Oh, and I don't want you giving that number out to anyone, even other cops who may be fans of mine," Recker said. "If someone else in the department calls me other than you, that phone's gonna be in the river the next day."

"No problem again. I figure the less I say about you the better it is for everyone."

"All right. Assuming there's no other problems, I'll probably call you again in a few days to let you know if I've come up with anything."

"Sounds good."

As soon as Recker hung up, he put the phone in his pocket and leaned forward on the desk to get a better view of the computer screen. He read each news story Jones found on the killing. After the fourth and final article, he took a seat next to Jones and

Haley and began discussing the case, as well as their options.

"Why didn't you see this earlier?" Recker asked. His tone was not accusing in nature or suggesting Jones wasn't on top of things, but just a simple question. "You're usually right on this type of stuff."

"Because quite honestly I wasn't looking for it. So far, my entire morning was spent digging into any further action against Judge Rocco."

Recker nodded. "Well, I guess me and Chris can dig through the police records of the two officers and see what we can find if you wanna stay on top of the Rocco stuff."

"Maybe one of us should sit on her home for a while," Haley said, mindful of the latest threat against the judge and wary of leaving her without the protection of one of them.

Recker agreed, though he wasn't sure they needed to sit on it all day. He looked at the time before replying. "Well if she's in court all day, she's not likely to get home until what? Six, seven, eight, something like that?"

Jones looked at him, unsure who he was asking the question to. It didn't sound like Recker was talking to anyone in particular. "Are you by chance asking me to check on her itinerary?"

Recker smiled. "Crossed my mind."

Jones rolled his eyes before swiveling back to the computer. "Very well. Since you asked so nicely."

Recker laughed to himself as Jones began checking Judge Rocco's court log. While he was doing that, Haley was still a bit uncomfortable with the situation. He thought they should have been on the judge more. Maybe even tail her as she left the courtroom.

"What if they try to knock her off or something on her way home?" Haley asked.

Recker shook his head, sure of his answer before he even said it. "They're not gonna try to kill her. Like we said, killing her does them no good. They'll just assign another judge. Can't kill all of them."

Jones was still listening even as he was doing his computer work. "Besides that, U.S. Marshals are providing protection for her on the way home."

"No, they don't want to hurt her," Recker said. "They wanna scare her, intimidate her. That's what they wanted to do by kidnapping her child. Let her know they could get to her, get to her family."

"So maybe they'll go after the kid again," Haley said.

"No, the messages I intercepted specifically made mention to the judge," Jones replied. "Nothing was said about the child. I believe the incident at the park has made them wary of that again. They probably believe the child already has security nearby when they go outside. It'd be a worthless effort to try that again."

"Well if the Marshals are going to be outside her house, what else could they try?" Haley asked. "And if they're stationed there, what good would we do? They've already got it staked out."

"No, they are not being stationed there. The judge has only requested security to and from the courtroom. They will not be outside her door all night."

"I'm assuming she has some type of alarm system?"

Jones nodded. "That would be correct. But we all know that's no real deterrent to a professional who knows what he's doing."

Recker sought to put his friend's mind at ease. He knew how frustrating these things could be at times. He felt it too from time to time and probably more often. "Don't worry. Whatever they're planning, we'll put a stop to it," he said, nodding at Haley. "We'll be there."

10

Recker and Haley had been watching Judge Rocco's house for over an hour. They weren't only waiting for the judge to get home, but also to see if she had any strange visitors come to the house. Haley was stationed near the front of the house, while Recker was in the back. Since the backyard of the house backed up to the property of a house behind it, there weren't many places for Recker to hide out and wait. He had to get into the backyard. There was a very small storage shed he had broken into as he watched the house.

"Getting anything out there yet?" Recker asked.

"No, all clear. You know, why doesn't she just invest in a personal bodyguard? Seems like it'd be a good idea."

"I don't know. I guess some people just feel like it's an intrusion or they don't need it."

"Well, after what happened the other day with her daughter I'd say it's necessary," Haley said.

"Well she's got protection now, and she's using it. That's why I think whatever's going down is gonna happen inside that house. They've gotta know she's got marshals protecting her now on the outside."

About ten minutes later, the judge arrived at her home, escorted by members of the U.S. Marshal's service. Haley alerted Recker to their presence so he'd know. They accompanied her to the door, and one man went inside the house with her. Once she was safely inside, the rest of the men went back to their car. They waited a few minutes just to make sure there were no problems then left once the coast seemed clear.

Haley immediately notified Recker, letting him know a man went inside with her. "Who do you think it is?"

"I dunno. Either one of the marshals or she's now got a personal security guard," Recker answered.

"I thought she thought it wasn't necessary."

"Maybe she changed her mind."

"Well it seems she's got things covered now."

"We'll see."

"Seeing as she's got someone in there with her, think we should pull out?" Haley asked.

"Nah. We're already here. Might as well see it through."

A little over a half hour after Judge Rocco returned home, the nanny then left. Once again, Haley gave his partner the heads up. Recker figured whatever might happen would take a while. He assumed it would be pitch black out before someone tried to sneak into the house. He periodically checked in with Jones to keep him informed of what was happening on their end, as well as seeing if he had learned anything new. Even as the two Silencers were outside the house, Jones was still feverishly checking to gain any new knowledge of the plot he'd uncovered.

As the night wore on, they didn't see any signs of danger. Nobody even came close to approaching the house, in either the front or the back. But there was a nagging feeling that kept tugging at Recker as he watched the house. There were still several lights on in the house, which seemed unusual to him. He knew from what Jones told him she had a full court schedule tomorrow. Recker figured she would have gone to bed as soon as possible with that schedule in mind. He watched the house for another half hour before calling Jones to tell him of his suspicions.

"David, what time did you say the judge usually leaves in the morning?"

"From what I can gather she is usually out of the house by seven-thirty," Jones answered. "Why do you ask?"

Recker hesitated for a moment, not even sure in his own mind what was bothering him. "I don't know. Something seems weird here."

"Such as?"

Recker let out a deep and audible sigh, indicating his uncertainty. "I don't know. I can't put my finger on it. Something just seems off."

Jones stopped what he was doing to fully concentrate on Recker's issue. "You are going to have to expand on that slightly, Mike. What exactly are you seeing or hearing?"

"Well, there's still several lights on in the house."

Jones didn't immediately reply, taking a few seconds to think. "And why is that a problem?"

"I dunno. Just seems like a judge who's got a full schedule tomorrow, with a baby in tow, would be going to sleep by now. But there's still at least three lights on that I can see."

Jones took a few more seconds to think, trying to analyze what he'd just been told. "Well let's look at it logically. She has a six-month-old baby. It could be that she's not asleep because the baby's not asleep."

"Possibly," Recker said.

"And she is a judge with a full plate tomorrow, as you said. It could be that she's staying up late to review the upcoming cases she has. Perhaps she is just studying. I know you always try to find the darker side of everything, but sometimes things are exactly what they appear to be."

"Yeah, maybe."

Jones then remembered that a man went inside with the judge when she came home. "Didn't you also state that a guard was with her?"

"Well, I didn't state it, but yeah."

"Maybe he's making his rounds," Jones said. "Maybe he doesn't want the house to be dark. Maybe he's just being extra cautious."

"Or maybe something's wrong."

This time it was Jones' turn to sigh. He knew no matter what he said, or could say, nothing was going to satisfy his friend. He was always going to think the worst. It was just Recker's nature.

"Can I just ask why you assume none of what I said is the case?" Jones asked. "Why does your mind automatically turn to the worst-case scenario?"

"Because it usually is."

"What do you propose to do?"

"I dunno. You know what else is bothering me?"

"I'm sure you'll explain."

"With some of those lights being on, I haven't seen anyone pass by," Recker said. "Not even a shadow."

"And so, I'll ask again, what do you propose to do?"

"I think I wanna go in."

Jones squirmed in his seat, envisioning a whole lot of ways that could go wrong. Dozens of thoughts went through his mind, all of which ended up badly for his team. Though he was hesitant to agree right away with Recker and give his blessing for them to enter the house, Jones did trust his instincts. No matter what the situation, Recker wasn't often wrong. Even when he didn't have much to go on, Recker's intuition was usually right on the money. Especially when he was the one in the field. It was tough for Jones to gauge sometimes how bad a situation was sitting from his chair. He wanted to get Haley's opinion before anything was officially decided, not that it necessarily guaranteed anything, as Recker could decide to go in no matter what anyone else said. Even so, Jones liked to gather all the facts from as many sources as possible before anything happened.

"Chris, have you been listening to what Mike and I have been discussing?"

"Yep."

"And what is your take on it? Have you noticed anything suspicious on your end?" Jones asked.

"Uh, I dunno. I mean, what Mike says makes sense. But then again, what you say makes sense too."

"What're you, playing Switzerland?" Recker asked.

Haley laughed. "I could see both scenarios being right."

"And how do you plan on getting in there?" Jones asked, expecting some type of elaborate plan.

Recker had a much simpler answer, though. "There's a back door."

"Oh, yes, how foolish of me to expect something else."

Just as they were about to agree on Recker and Haley moving in to check out the house, Jones thought of a different plan. He thought it was a much easier and simpler idea.

"Hold up on storming the house," Jones said.

"Why?" Recker asked.

"I've got a better way. I've got the judge's phone number right here. I'll just give her a call. If she answers, we'll know she's fine. If not, then maybe something's up."

Recker wasn't as impressed with the idea. "I've got a couple of comebacks on that."

"Go on."

"What if she is one of those people who doesn't answer the phone if she doesn't know the number calling?"

"I guess that's a thought."

"Or what if she answers and somebody actually is there and makes her answer in a way that makes it seem as though everything is fine?"

Jones could see that his simpler and easier idea was about to go by the wayside. "You've made your point."

"Or what if she actually is sleeping and just forgot to turn out the lights?"

"I said you made your point."

"I was just throwing out a few retorts," Recker said.

"Yes, yes, I get the gist of it."

"So, no matter what happens with that phone call of yours, it might not really mean or change anything."

"I understand that. I hear what you're saying."

"If someone is in there, though, it might give them a warning. They might think she was expecting a call and put them on high alert."

"I'm taking it that you think we should just bypass the phone call?"

"I think we'd be better off."

After a few more minutes of discussion, it was agreed upon that Recker and Haley would stay put for a little while longer to see if anything changed. Once midnight struck, they were given the go-ahead to move in. The time moved by quickly, and without seeing any type of movement inside the house, Recker was ready to go. Before moving, he coordinated plans with Haley.

"I'll go in first through the back," Recker said.

"Where do you want me to go?"

"Just sit tight for a minute until I give you the word. If there's nothing wrong, then I don't want both of us struggling to get out of there. If I come across anything, I'll let you know and you come in."

"Right," Haley replied.

Recker exited the small shed he was stationed in and approached the back door of the house, running over to it as fast as he could. Once there, he picked the lock and had the door open in under a minute. As he walked inside the house, he withdrew his gun, ready to fire if necessary. He walked through a dark area which appeared to be some type of storage room. He cleared a couple other rooms, letting Jones and Haley know his findings up to that point. Recker then found some steps that led up to a door and what he assumed was the main part of the house.

Recker gently turned the knob on the door and

slowly opened it, peeking at what was on the other side. One of the lights was on and as Recker closed the door behind him, observed that it was the main living area. To the left of him was the kitchen, and Recker retreated to it to make sure nobody could come up behind him. Once he knew it to be empty, he went back to the living room, keeping his guard up the entire time. He peeked into the room to make sure no one was around the corner then cautiously walked into the middle of the room. To his far right were steps that led up to the bedrooms. He didn't need to see anything else, though, to know that something was definitely wrong.

At the bottom of the steps was a man lying on the floor face down, his wrists tied together against the staircase. Recker assumed he wasn't dead, or he wouldn't have needed to be tied up, but went over to him just to make sure. The man was still breathing, but he had a nasty bump on his head, and some blood on the back of his skull thanks to a nice-sized gash. Recker looked up the stairs but didn't see or hear anything coming from that direction. Still, he knew something had to be up there. They had both entrances covered, and nobody had left. Before going ahead, he let the others know what he encountered.

"Is it the security guard?" Jones asked.

"I don't know. I didn't see him. I'll take a picture of his face and send it to Chris."

Recker quickly pulled out his phone and snapped a

picture of the man's face and sent it to Haley for confirmation. If it was the security guard, it was a clear sign the judge was in trouble. If it turned out not to be the guard, then it led to the possibility it was an intruder the guard took care of and had the judge in a more secure location. If that was the case, they didn't have long to wait as it was likely the police would have been notified by now. If that was true, they risked staying there, and getting trapped.

Luckily, Haley recognized the face instantly. "That's the guard," he said.

"All right, get in here," Recker replied.

Haley got out of his car and ran across the street. Like Recker, he got through the door in less than a minute. He quickly found Recker in the living room. They agreed that once they got up the stairs, they'd split up and take different rooms. When they got to the top of the steps, Recker went to his left as Haley took the right. Recker's first room was what looked like a spare bedroom. It was very neat and orderly, and looked like it hadn't been used much. As he was checking, Haley's door opened into the baby's room. He quickly cleared it, then walked over to the crib to see if the baby was inside. She was sleeping.

"Baby's in her crib," Haley said.

"She OK?" Recker asked.

"Yep. Sleeping like a baby."

"Ha," Jones said, appreciating the humor. "How à propos."

After exiting his room, Recker went down the hall to the next door. He thought he heard something and put his ear against the door to listen. He heard a man talking. It didn't sound like a pleasant conversation, as the man's voice kept raising; he wasn't happy about something. As Haley was checking out another room, Recker started turning the handle on the door, ready to burst in on the discussion.

Recker forcefully pushed the door open and immediately saw the judge sitting in a chair tied up with a gag in her mouth. He then noticed a man standing to her right with a gun in his hand. As soon as the man saw the stranger come into the room, he pulled his gun up to fire. Recker, though, beat him to the punch and raised his own weapon. Recker pointed at the man and immediately fired, pulling the trigger twice. Both shots lodged into the man's chest, knocking him onto the floor. Recker quickly scanned the rest of the room to see if the man had a partner, but there was no one else in sight.

"I got one down," Recker said. "Keep checking the rest of the house."

"I'm on it," Haley replied.

Recker walked over to the fallen man and stood over top of his lifeless body. With the amount of blood coming out of his shirt, and the range he was shot at, Recker figured he was dead. He reached down to check his pulse just to make sure. The man was dead. Recker took a careful look at his face and recognized him as the third member of the gang they were looking for. Then Recker looked back at the judge and walked over to her, removing her restraints. After she was untied, and the gag removed from her mouth, she felt and rubbed her wrists.

The judge looked up at the man who she assumed was a police officer, appreciative of his efforts. "Thank you."

"Glad I could help."

She then remembered her protection and stood. "My security guard, he got hit in the head."

Recker put his hand out to let her know to relax. "He's fine. He's got a nasty bump, but he'll be OK."

"Oh, thank God."

"My baby..."

"You're baby's fine. Still in her crib sleeping, not a care in the world," Recker said with a smile.

A look of relief swept across Rocco's face as she sat back down. "I don't know what happened. It all happened so fast."

"Well, we've been watching your house for a while and didn't see him come in, so he must've already been here waiting for you when you got home."

Rocco looked puzzled. "You've been watching my house? Why?"

"We got word that something might happen."

"Word? Why wasn't I notified?"

Recker shrugged, drawing another curious look from the judge. "We don't usually do that."

"What district are you with?" Rocco asked.

Recker shook his head. "I'm not with the police."

"What? Who are you, then? What are you doing here?"

"Just helping where I'm needed," Recker answered.

Rocco looked at his face a little closer, studying it. It was a face that looked familiar to her somehow, though she couldn't place it at first. "Have you been in my courtroom before?"

Recker smiled, thankful he couldn't say he had. "No."

"I've seen you somewhere before."

"I get that a lot."

Haley then reported back after checking the rest of the rooms. "Rest of the house is clear."

"All right, I'll meet you back outside," Recker replied.

"Who are you talking to?" Rocco asked.

"I have friends."

Rocco continued studying his face. She knew she'd seen it before. She was positive of it. After another minute, she snapped her fingers as it came to her. "I've got it."

"You do?"

"You're him."

Recker knew what she was referring to, but chose to make light out of it instead, not wanting to make a big deal of it. "Well I've never been called a her so that's a good start."

Rocco smiled. "You're the Silencer, aren't you?"

Recker looked away for a second, not really giving any type of confirmation or denial. He didn't need to give one in either direction, though. The judge already knew it was true.

"Why the special interest in me?" she asked.

Recker looked perplexed, not sure of her meaning. "Special interest?"

"I was told you also intervened at the park the other day. I guess I also have you to thank for that."

Recker shrugged, not looking for thanks. "Just glad I was able to get there in time to stop it."

Rocco looked at him and smiled again. "So, you're the famous vigilante. You know, I've always thought we might meet one day."

"Oh?"

"Yes, but I always assumed it'd be while I was wearing my robe and you'd be in handcuffs."

Recker let out a slight laugh. "Sorry to disappoint you."

"Well, as thankful as I am for helping me and my daughter, I have to say it wouldn't help you if you do find yourself in that situation."

"Didn't think it would."

"I mean, if you ever do wind up in my courtroom, I'd have to throw the book at you."

Recker smiled, not at all bothered by the warning. "I'd hope for and expect nothing less."

Rocco then gave him a wink. "But let's hope it never comes to that."

Recker nodded. "I can agree with that."

"How do you do what you do?"

"Trade secrets."

The judge nodded, not wanting to pry too much into his affairs. Though they were technically on opposite sides, and due to her profession, she was officially against what he did, Rocco was grateful for his assistance in helping her family. But she was a person of integrity, and if Recker ever did show up in her court, she couldn't do much for him. As much as Recker was enjoying the conversation, he knew he had to be going. Sticking around any longer would be risky.

"Well, I'll let you get back to your business," Recker said. "I'll have the police called in a few minutes."

Rocco blinked and nodded. "Thank you. I certainly hope I never have to see you again. In any setting."

"That makes two of us."

"Before you go, can I ask you a personal question?"

"Sure."

"Why do you do it? All this. You know it will probably end badly for you. Do you do it for kicks? Notoriety? Money? What?"

"Honestly, I just do it 'cause I wanna help people. Don't give a damn about money, fame, or anything else. The only thing I get out of it is the satisfaction of helping people and making sure they're safe. That's all."

"So that's really all there is to it?"

"That's really it."

"What'd you do before this?"

"Why the third degree?" Recker asked.

Rocco shrugged. "Just curious. You're a polarizing figure. Just wondering what makes you tick."

"Before this I worked for the government in various situations overseas. Didn't end so well for me. But don't go looking me up. You won't find anything."

The judge just nodded and gave a faint smile. "I kind of figured that would be the case."

"You stay safe."

"You figure this is the last of this type of stuff against me?"

"Well, there was a three-person crew contracted to work against you," Recker said. "Two are locked up, and this one's killed, so I think that should be the end of it. We'll keep an ear out just in case they come up with something new, but I've got a feeling they'll get the hint that this isn't gonna work."

"You said we, there's more of you?"

Recker smiled, but wasn't about to divulge anything else. "Let's just say that I'm not alone."

11

———

It'd been a week since Recker and company saved
Judge Rocco from the break-in of the last
remaining crew member they had been watching. Jones had kept tabs on the judge, typing in a few
extra parameters into his search engine to see if he
could uncover any further heinous attempts to side-
track her in an upcoming trial. As far as he could tell,
she was in the clear. After two failed attempts, the
powers that be behind the attacks had nothing else
they were working on.

With the judge no longer an issue, Recker and
Haley focused on other cases, neither of them working
together on any assignment since then. They were
both busy, though, each having at least one assignment
a day, and on a couple of occasions, two or three. There
were several robbery attempts, kidnappings, a few
planned murders, as well as an arson attempt, and a

couple of planned assaults. After the busy week, and with their slate of cases currently empty, Recker had planned to sleep late one morning. He took turns with Haley, who slept in the day before. He didn't come in until twelve, which was around the time Recker was planning on coming in. Mia had a late shift that day and Recker was planning on spending the morning with her. Unfortunately, as it often did, his plans didn't work out the way he intended.

Though Recker got to sleep in a little, waking up at nine, the rest of the morning was not as quiet as he was hoping. He'd just finished eating breakfast with Mia when his phone started ringing. When he got to the table and saw who it was, he looked up at the ceiling and let out a deep sigh, knowing his morning was about to be cut short. Whenever Jones was calling at a time when Recker was supposed to be off, if there ever was such a thing, it meant something major had just happened and his private time was coming to an end. Before answering, he looked over at Mia, who gave him a faint smile, also recognizing what the call would probably mean.

"Hey, what's up?"

"Sorry to do this to you," Jones said. "I know you were looking forward to having the morning to yourselves."

"It's fine. What's going on?"

"Bad news I'm afraid. It appears that another police officer has been shot and killed."

"How?" Recker asked.

"Walking out of his house last night on the way to begin his shift. He did the overnight watch."

"It's been what, week and a half, two weeks since the last one?"

"Yes. And our special phone rang this morning and has a voicemail on it from our detective friend," Jones said.

"You didn't answer it?"

"I think the less he knows about our business the better. He only knows you, only has dealt with you, I think we should keep it that way."

"Yeah, probably right about that. You listen to the message?" Recker asked.

"I did. It was basically just going over a few details of this shooting and asking you to call him back when you could."

"Have you been able to look into it yet?"

"Well, thankfully we've got a little lull in our case log right now, so I was able to check a few things out so far. Haven't got too deep into it yet, but it's still early."

"Any connections to the other victims?"

"No," Jones said. "Once again, he worked in a different district, no obvious relationship to the other officers."

Recker stayed silent for a few moments, the phone still pressed to his ear, as he tried to think of their next move.

Jones hoped his silence meant he thought of something. "Come up with anything?"

Recker let out a sigh, not sure if he did or not. He had something, whether it was any good or not, was still to be decided. "I don't know yet. Cops are going down every week. I think it's time we stepped things up a notch."

"What do you mean?"

"We need to get active about this. We've been pretty passive over it."

"Well, to be fair, it is a police matter and they've been investigating it themselves," Jones said.

"Obviously hasn't meant much."

"We have also had our own things to work on."

"I know, I know. I'm just saying, now, we need to ramp it up."

"And what do you have in mind?"

"Tyrell hasn't reported back with anything. How about if we give him pictures of the three cops that were killed, not in uniform, and see if he can start knocking some doors down?" Recker answered.

"I suppose we could do that."

"And I wanna have another chat with Vincent."

"Can I ask what for?" Jones asked, not seeing what good that would do.

"He might know something."

"Excuse me for being argumentative, but he already inquired about it once before, did he not? When he first introduced you to Detective Andrews?"

"Yeah."

"I guess I don't understand what the point of it would be."

"He didn't know at the time who was behind it," Recker said. "That doesn't mean he might not know what the connection is."

Jones hesitated before replying. "I guess I can see what you mean. But that is also supposing that there is a connection to be found."

"Yeah, it is."

"It might just be some random lunatic."

"I'm guessing no," Recker said.

"Why?"

"I dunno. The more I think about it, the more it seems like something that's planned."

"Even lunatics have moments of clarity, Mike."

"I know. But when cops are shot walking out of their house, to me, that shows they were targeted. Those people specifically. Not cops in general. If it was just some random person going on a rampage, I don't think he'd be sitting and waiting outside their house, assuming he even knew where they lived. He would just wait for a parked patrol car or something, create a false call they'd have to roll on, something like that."

"I might be able to go along with that," Jones replied.

"Start working on those pictures and I'll call Vincent to set something up."

"OK. If I can't find anything, then I'll just digitally

alter their police profile pictures and make it look like they're not wearing a uniform."

"Whatever's faster for you."

As soon as Recker hung up, he glanced at Mia, who was sitting on the couch. She had the TV on, but she wasn't paying much attention to it. But she was listening to what her boyfriend was saying. And she didn't like it very much. Recker could tell by the scowl on her face and the unfriendly stare she was giving him, that something wasn't sitting well with her.

"What's that look for?"

"Hmm? Oh, nothing."

"Mia? I know that look. Something's bothering you, just tell me what it is."

She quickly relented, not wanting to get into a long, drawn out give-and-take with him. Especially since he always found out what was bothering her, anyway. "It's just I heard you say you were going to meet with Vincent."

Recker batted his eyes for a moment, not understanding what the issue was. "So?"

"You know I hate it when you meet with him."

Recker sat next to her and put his arms around her. "You know sometimes I have to."

"I just don't trust him. I'm always afraid he's going to double-cross you somehow."

Recker smiled, then planted a kiss on her cheek. "Believe me, he's not gonna double-cross me. If he was going to, he'd have done it long before now."

"You're acting like he's a moral person or something. He is a criminal you know."

"I know that. Trust me. I'll be fine."

"You'll take Chris along as backup?"

Recker rolled his eyes, but agreed with her request, even if he wasn't positive the other Silencer would be tagging along. "Yes, I'll take Chris along."

He took a few more minutes to put Mia's mind at ease, then called Malloy to set up a meeting with Vincent. Luckily, the crime boss was willing to meet with him in about an hour. He had to go to the office first before the meeting, so he couldn't hang out with Mia much longer.

"Make it up to you later," Recker said.

"It's OK," she replied, after getting a kiss on the cheek. "Want me to bring dinner home?"

"You're working late."

"Well, something tells me you'll be working late too."

Recker smiled. "You know me too well."

Recker took a few minutes to get himself together, then gave Mia a goodbye kiss before heading to the office. When he got there, Jones and Haley were both sitting at the desk working. Recker walked around to the front of the desk, facing them.

"You print out those pictures yet?" Recker asked.

Jones nodded, then reached for a folder on the desk and handed it to him. Recker opened the folder and saw five four by six pictures, three of the cops, one of the drug dealer, and the one they assumed to be the innocent victim.

"Meeting at the restaurant?" Jones asked.

"No, at the trucking place," Recker replied.

"Are you really hoping he will tell you something?"

"Not hoping for anything. Just ticking off the boxes. Maybe something will come of it."

"Want me to go along?" Haley asked.

Recker briefly thought of Mia when he asked the question, but he knew there was no reason for backup. He and Vincent were on good enough terms where he didn't even have to entertain the thought of something going wrong. Plus, saving Vincent's life should have been enough to earn Recker a lifetime pass from him. Though he knew he was technically breaking his promise, he knew it just wasn't necessary. If there was even a one percent chance, Recker would've agreed to let Haley come along as backup. But with things as they were, he felt Haley was better off working on other things.

"No, I'll be fine," Recker said. "We got anything else in the hopper?"

"Yes, but nothing that's critical enough to warrant both of you being on it," Jones answered. "Chris can take care of it."

"What is it?"

"There's a man threatening his ex-girlfriend."

"How bad?"

Jones shrugged, not knowing how to answer. "How

bad are these things usually? There's a threat that's severe enough for us to act on. Don't worry about it. I'll put Chris on it. Concentrate on your business with Vincent."

Recker agreed and looked at the photos in the folder again. It also had information about each of the victims. As he glanced at the contents, Jones wondered about a few things Recker mentioned to him previously.

"What about Tyrell? When was the last time you heard from him?"

"Five or six days I guess," Recker answered.

"Are you still sending him the pictures?"

"Oh, yeah, I almost forgot about that. I'll give him a call now and see what's up."

Recker immediately called Tyrell, who answered on the second ring.

"Hey, what's up?"

"Just wondering if you've made any progress on that police thing we talked about?" Recker asked.

"Nah, not so far. Nobody seems like they're that interested in talking."

"Kinda figured that'd be the case. I'm gonna email you some pictures. Flash them around, see if anybody recognizes them."

"Will do."

After his conversation with Tyrell ended, Recker took a few more minutes to read some of the files on the fallen police officers. He got so caught up in what he was looking at he almost forgot the time. Once he looked at the clock on the wall, he quickly shuffled the papers back into the folder.

"I need to get going," Recker said.

Recker walked out of the office and headed for Vincent's trucking business. When he got there, the front gates were already open, with a few trucks pulling in and out of the premises. Recker usually was only there at nighttime, when most of the business was done for the day. He had almost forgotten there was an actual business in operation. The security guard was already given instructions to clear Recker when he got there. Recker pulled into a parking spot and headed into the facilities. It was only a minute or two until Malloy greeted him.

"Does he ever go anywhere without you?" Recker asked.

Malloy just smiled. "Not usually."

Recker looked out the window at several trucks coming in and out. "Bustling place."

"It has its moments."

"Almost forgot that this place had an actual business purpose during the daytime."

Malloy led Recker through the warehouse, and down the hallway, until they reached the office door. Malloy opened the door and let Recker in, revealing Vincent sitting at the desk. Recker glanced at the décor, but it looked the same as it always did. Vincent was writing something in a notebook, then stopped and tossed the pen down on the desk as he put eyes on his visitor. He closed the book as Recker sat across from him. Malloy closed the door behind him and leaned up against the wall to the side of the two men. Vincent leaned back and put his elbows on the arm of the chair and clasped his hands together.

"Jimmy told me there was something you wanted to talk about."

"Yeah. Thanks for agreeing to meet so soon," Recker said.

"No problem. The least I could do for you. Usually when you request something, there's a certain urgency involved."

"I wanted to talk about the problem you got me involved in."

"The problem I got you involved in?" Vincent asked, not sure where he was going with the question.

"Meeting your law enforcement friend, getting caught up in his situation."

"Well that was hardly my problem. I was simply the middleman. You were free to help or not help as you saw fit."

By the face that Recker replied with, Vincent could tell that he wasn't making much progress on the case.

"I take it that it's been giving you fits," Vincent said.

"I guess that's one way of putting it. You still don't have any information on it?"

Vincent shook his head. "If I knew of anything, you wouldn't even be here right now. I would've given that information to Detective Andrews already. That would've eliminated the need for you."

"You know all the people killed so far, right?"

"Yes, three officers and two civilians if I'm not mistaken."

"One of them was a low-level drug dealer," Recker said.

"I'm sure you have a point with that."

"Well, you have control over this entire city now. I would think that you would have information on anybody active in this town. No matter how small."

Vincent made a face and shrugged. "And you think I know of every single person who's doing something illegal?"

"I would be surprised if you didn't."

"Well then I guess you will be surprised to know that I don't lay the hammer down a hundred percent. I don't concern myself with small-time dealers and criminals. They're small time for a reason."

"You just let anyone operate on your turf without being checked?" Recker asked.

"I'm more concerned with the bigger picture. I don't need to know every single detail that's going on out there. I think that's where men in power get tripped up sometimes. They worry about things that aren't especially meaningful. If there's a few hoods out there dealing drugs or weapons, I'm fine with it. If they stay small and are only putting money in their own pocket; food on their table. It's when they have bigger ambitions and start taking it out of my pocket that I'll have an issue with it."

"And everybody knows that?"

"Most do. If they don't, then someone will put them in line."

Recker pulled out his folder and put it on the desk, sliding it over to Vincent.

"What's this?"

"Pictures, names, information of the deceased," Recker replied. "I know you said you don't know anything, but I thought maybe if you saw the names, looked at the faces, maybe something would ring a bell."

Vincent grabbed the folder and held it above the desk and opened it. "Fair enough."

Recker silently looked on as Vincent looked through the contents of the folder. The boss took several minutes, giving it an honest effort. With almost anyone else who might have been there, Vincent likely would have just given it a cursory look and not put much effort into it. But to continue the goodwill they had with each other, Vincent genuinely tried to recall seeing any of the names or faces. Before Recker slid the folder to him, he hadn't seen either. He only knew the situation based on news reports and what he'd been told. He didn't concern himself with the names at that point. After several minutes, Vincent shook his head and closed the folder.

"Afraid I can't help you. None of the faces look

familiar. I haven't come across any of these names before either."

Recker could see he was being given an honest answer. Vincent wasn't giving him some fluff or anything. There was another question on his mind, and he hoped Vincent wouldn't take umbrage at it.

"None of these officers were on your payroll, were they? No offense meant."

Vincent smiled. "No, they were not. And no offense taken."

"Just figured I'd ask."

"If they were on my payroll, don't you think I'd have some knowledge of what was going on?"

"Maybe. Or maybe they weren't paid well enough for you to care."

"Fair enough. In any case it's a moot point since they're not."

"I guess there's one more question that has to be asked," Recker said.

"Well, I think I might be able to anticipate what that question is, but you go ahead anyway."

"You're not behind this, are you?"

"What do you think?"

"I'd say it was unlikely, but like I said, the question has to be asked."

"Then my answer would be no, I'm not. If I was, do you really think I would reach out to get you involved to investigate? That would be a pretty stupid thing to do on my part considering how well you do your job."

"Not talking of you specifically, but, generally speaking, people do stupid things all the time."

"Agreed. But I am not one of those people," Vincent said.

"No doubt about it. Well, you made an effort," Recker said. "That's all I could ask."

Vincent, trying to help him and offer something useful, slid the folder to the side of the desk, pointed in Malloy's direction.

"Jimmy? Take a look if you will."

"Sure," Malloy said, moving toward the desk.

Malloy did as his boss did and looked at the pictures carefully. Once he was done with them, he moved on to the names and information of the victims. After he gave it a few minutes, he had the same response as Vincent. He put everything back in the folder and handed it to Recker.

"Don't know any of them either."

Recker sighed in frustration, though he wasn't too surprised. "I won't take up any more of your time."

"Sorry we couldn't be of help," Vincent said.

"Figured it was worth a shot."

"Just out of curiosity, what do your instincts tell you?"

"My instincts?"

"Yes. Surely you have some thoughts or theories about what's going on, whether you can prove them or actually have any proof to lead you to it."

Recker's eyes darted around the room for a few

seconds as he pondered the question. Vincent was right. He did have some thoughts he really hadn't shared until now. He tried not to offer any ideas about anything he at least didn't have some evidence that would lead him in the right direction.

"So far there's no link that connects any of these people together."

"But you feel there is one?" Vincent asked.

"I do. I kind of doubt five people being shot in a matter of weeks is random. Could it be? Sure. I just have a tough time believing it."

"What would the connection be?"

"I don't know. The dealer, the innocent victim, and the undercover officer were all shot in proximity to one another. That leads me to believe something happened that wasn't supposed to be seen. Or something happened that wasn't supposed to."

"And the other officers?"

"Cops being shot outside their houses indicates a personal connection," Recker said.

"And what does that lead you to?"

"It leads me to believe that maybe they were involved in something they shouldn't have been."

Vincent nodded, having the same feeling. "Perhaps you're right."

Recker left the office and drove out of the lot. He let Jones know nothing came of the meeting. Even though he believed Vincent didn't know anything, something was tugging at Recker that he knew more. Maybe it was just his cynical nature. But it almost seemed to him Vincent was trying to lead him down the path that Recker eventually stumbled upon without saying anything. But like most things with Vincent, Recker could never be completely sure of anything. He would just have to hope Tyrell would have better luck.

12

Another week went by with two more shootings of police officers. Both officers were killed walking out of their houses. With not having anything new to work with, Recker was willing to do just about anything to get the crucial piece of evidence they needed to find out who the shooter was. Right now, he'd settle for just knowing what the connection to all the officers was. And he knew there had to be one. The growing sentiment amongst the police, according to Andrews, was the attacks were random, and there was no link between any of them. It was a belief shared by Jones, and even Haley was starting to come around to that line of thinking. Recker seemed to be the last holdout. It was possible he'd eventually be proven wrong, but he just couldn't make himself think some crazy person was going around shooting cops. He knew there had to be more to it than that.

With that desperation in mind, Recker called for a meeting with Tyrell at Charlie's Bar. The place didn't open until four, but Recker had called and asked him if he could use a table. As Charlie always got there at one to start setting up for the night, and that Recker was always welcome anytime, he had no problem in letting the Silencer use his establishment. It was two o'clock, and Recker and Haley had arrived right on schedule. While they were waiting, Charlie brought a couple of drinks over for the two men.

"Here's a couple of sodas for you gents," Charlie said, putting the two glasses down.

"Thanks, Charlie," Recker replied.

"Ah, no sweat, boys."

As soon as Charlie walked away, Haley took a sip of his drink. "Wonder what's keeping him."

"I dunno. He's usually not late."

A few more minutes went by before they heard a tap on the wood of the front door. Charlie walked over to it, and after quizzing the visitor, let him in. Tyrell walked over to the table and sat across from his friends.

"Took you long enough," Recker said, not letting go of the opportunity to kid him.

"Hey man, I hit traffic."

A minute later, Charlie came by with another drink, putting in front of Tyrell. "I'll leave you boys to your discussion. If you need anything else, just give me a holler. I'll be in the back."

"Thanks, Charlie," Recker said.

Tyrell took a drink, then stood and removed his jacket. Recker looked at it closely as Tyrell slung it over the back of his chair.

"That new?" Recker asked.

Tyrell took a look behind him at the jacket before answering. "Yeah. Just got it a couple days ago."

"Nice. Looks shiny."

"Genuine leather."

Recker looked at the jacket again, then Tyrell. He opened his mouth and was about to make a joke, but Tyrell put his hand up to stop him from going any further.

"Listen, man, I like the jacket. It's comfortable. I can do without any of your sarcastic responses."

Recker smiled and let out a laugh, unable to contain himself. "All right, let's get down to business then."

"Before we start that, can I just say how weird it is that there's two of you now?"

Recker and Haley looked at each other, neither of whom thought there was anything weird about it.

"Why?" Recker asked.

"I dunno. For so long I was just dealing with one of you running around, saving the city. Now there's two of you. I dunno. Just don't seem natural."

"This isn't the first time you two have met."

"I know. I was just sayin'. I just can't believe there's two of you crazy mo-fo's running around the city now, playing superhero, stalking around in the middle of the night."

"We don't stalk around," Haley said, joking.

"And it's not always the middle of the night," Recker said.

"Yeah, yeah. So, what'd you want to meet about?"

"We wanna get more proactive about this police thing," Recker said. "Cops are dropping like crazy around here and we need to put a stop to it now."

Tyrell made a face, making Recker think he wasn't on board with the idea.

"What, you don't think so?"

Tyrell shrugged. "Nah, it's not that. But, I mean, I don't know what else we can do. You know I've checked around. Nobody's got nothin' to say. You know the cops have put everything they got on this. And Vincent, you checked with Vincent. Even he don't know what's going on. Now if I don't know, Vincent don't know, and the cops don't know... maybe there ain't nothin' to know."

Recker shook his head. "I just can't believe that. There's always somebody that knows something. There's always a piece of evidence out there some-where. We just have to find it."

"I dunno, man. I don't know where it is."

"Maybe it's like fishing. Maybe we just haven't used the right kind of bait."

"You know I don't fish," Tyrell said.

"If you wanna catch a different kind of fish, sometimes you gotta put a different kind of bait on the hook to reel them in."

"And what would that bait be?"

"Money," Recker answered.

"Money?"

"Yeah. So far, it hasn't been offered. You were just using your connections, Vincent wasn't really looking, and the cops don't bribe for information."

"Maybe not the ones you know," Tyrell said, scoffing at his suggestion. "I know a few who do."

"Regardless, the ones who are investigating this, don't."

"So whatcha you got in mind?"

Recker reached into his pocket and removed an envelope. He set it down and slid it across the table. Tyrell picked it up and looked inside. As he was holding the envelope, looking at the money that was inside, he peeked up at Recker.

"How much is in here?" Tyrell asked.

"Couple thousand."

"And I'm supposed to use this to get the answers we're looking for?"

Recker nodded. "That's the plan."

Tyrell folded the flap of the envelope back down and put it in the pocket of his jacket. "And you think this is the right kind of bait?"

"You don't?"

"I dunno. Beats me. I'm just asking."

"Can't hurt."

"How much of this am I supposed to use?"

"As much as you need," Recker answered.

"What makes you think this is gonna give you the answers you're looking for?"

"We all know money talks. Maybe people just haven't been motivated enough to give us what we need."

Tyrell slouched down in his chair and put his elbow on the arm of it and balled his hand into a fist as he rested it against the side of his mouth. He was contemplating the situation, and what he was being asked to do.

"Can I just ask why you're so dead set on thinking that this isn't the work of some whack job out there? Why does everything gotta be some conspiracy theory or something?"

Recker leaned over and made a grimace as he itched his side as he contemplated the question. "I dunno. I guess I just have a hard time believing this is the work of a crazy person."

"Why?"

"Just doesn't feel like it."

"Seriously? That's all you got? It just doesn't feel like it? Nothing specific to go on?"

Recker shook his head. "Nope. Just a hunch."

Tyrell rubbed his mouth with the palm of his hand. "And what are you gonna do if this doesn't pan out?"

"I don't know. Haven't thought about it. Guess we'll cross that bridge when we come to it."

Tyrell sighed, thinking this was gonna be a waste of time. He was willing to do it since he got paid for it no matter what, but based on his conversations with some of his contacts previously, he just didn't think they'd have anything more to share, even with money being thrown in their faces. But he was known to be wrong before with some of the people he dealt with, and Recker was right because money had a way of loosening lips sometimes.

"All right, I'll give it a shot," Tyrell said. "Hope we can turn something for you. I'll start working on it right away."

"Appreciate it."

Tyrell took one last sip of his drink then stood and put his new jacket on.

"Snazzy," Recker said.

"Hey, what'd I tell you about that?"

Recker laughed again. "Just couldn't resist a parting shot."

"Yeah, I bet. So, what do I do in the event I do find someone willing to talk, assuming there is such a person, and this ain't enough?" Tyrell said, tapping the envelope in his pocket.

"There's three thousand dollars in there. I think that should be plenty."

"Never know. I'm just asking."

"If you find someone who's looking for more, you let me know."

"I'll do that."

Tyrell started to leave but was interrupted by Recker, who had some last-minute instructions for him.

"Tyrell?"

"Yeah."

"Just don't be giving that money to anybody who might have information," Recker said. "They better have something, and it better be right, and it better be good."

Tyrell looked at him strangely, like he was talking to someone else. "What do you think I am? A rookie or something?"

Recker smiled at him. "I'm just saying."

Tyrell waved at him then left the bar. Recker and Haley stayed a few minutes longer to finish their drinks and discuss things a little more.

"You really think he's gonna come up with something?" Haley asked.

"I do. Wouldn't have done it if I didn't think it'd work."

"Well, sometimes people throw crap at the wall and hope that something sticks. Doesn't mean they believe that it will."

"I think Tyrell will find out something," Recker said. "He knows enough people that he'll find someone who'll start talking. I believe that someone knows something. Somebody has to."

They stayed another five minutes, then when their drinks were finished, started leaving. Recker went to the back office to let Charlie know they were going and to thank him for letting them use his place. When the two Silencers got back to the office, Jones had some news for them.

"Well, Tyrell's gonna hit the streets again," Recker said. "Armed with some extra funding, of course."

"We may not even need it," Jones said, typing away, not even bothering to look at them entering the office.

Recker's mood quickly perked up, thinking, and hoping his partner had found something. "Why? What's up?"

"I'm not sure but I may have found a common link. Nothing concrete yet, but it's a start."

"What'd you come up with?" Recker asked, sitting at the desk next to him, eagerly looking at the screen.

Haley also pulled up a chair, sitting just behind the two men, looking between their shoulders.

Jones finished up what he was typing before explaining. "Three months ago, Officer Jennings opened up a new bank account with a five-thousand-dollar deposit."

"OK?" Recker asked, not seeing a connection so far.

"Officer Bridges did the same thing three months ago."

"Nothing we can really pin down," Haley said.

Jones put his finger in the air, indicating he wasn't done yet. "Officer Wheaton opened up a new bank account six months ago."

"That's three," Recker said.

Jones still wasn't done. "And five months ago, Officer Clemont did the same."

"All with the same amount?" Haley asked.

Jones nodded. "All with the same amount. Five-thousand-dollar deposits."

"That is a pretty big coincidence."

"I'm still not done. None of these new accounts were opened up in those officer's names."

"Then whose were they?" Recker asked.

"Names of relatives. Mothers and wives mostly."

"How'd you pick up on it?"

Jones gave an unassuming shrug. "Well, nothing came up in their personnel packages or their records, so I just figured I would try to dig a little deeper. Jennings was the only one who did not open up an account in someone else's name."

"I wonder why?" Haley asked.

"Jennings was not married, and his parents were already deceased. He also was an only child, and he did not have any children of his own either."

"Oh."

"Figure out where that money came from?" Recker said.

"Unfortunately, no. They all deposited checks from a newly established security company. They all had the words 'Consulting' written in the memo line."

"Trying to make it look legitimate."

"Indeed," Jones replied. "But, I've checked the company's history and they are as phony as a three-dollar bill."

"Not a real company?"

"Fake name, fake owner, fake business account, all come back with dead ends."

"How about trying to get into the bank account footage?" Recker asked. "If we can get a picture of the guy opening the account, maybe we can hone in on him."

"Unfortunately, that is no longer possible."

"Why's that?" Haley asked.

"Because the bank only keeps their security footage for six months. There is nothing left to check."

"Figures."

"What about the bank account itself?" Recker said. "Can you get into it? Find any other transactions that might go somewhere."

"I've already been ahead of you. There are no other transactions, and while the account is still technically open, there is no longer any money in it."

"Damn."

"The account was opened a year ago with a small deposit of a thousand dollars. It was built up over the next three months until it reached a total of thirty thousand."

MIKE RYAN

Recker didn't need any further explaining to know what that meant. Thirty thousand dollars, six officers, five thousand each. The account was opened specifically to pay them in a manner which would not draw suspicion. If it was investigated, it would seem they were being paid consulting work by a security firm, which was not unusual work or behavior for cops who were looking for a part-time or side gig.

"Seems pretty clear that something's going on here," Haley said.

Recker and Jones both agreed with the assessment, though neither voiced it right away. Recker always had that hunch anyway, so it wasn't exactly a surprise for him. But it was the link, the one piece of evidence they'd been looking for that confirmed his suspicion. After a few minutes of silence, Recker looked over at the computer genius.

"Well? What do you think now?"

"I would say that you were right," Jones answered, shuffling a few papers around. "I would say that is definitely a link."

"And a shady one at that."

"What now?" Haley asked.

"We keep digging until we hit gold."

"Perhaps it would be wise to let our detective friend know about this," Jones said. "Assuming he doesn't already. Maybe he could shed more light on it."

Though Recker wasn't sure Andrews could tell them more than they already knew, he agreed to call him anyway, just to cover all the bases. After a few rings, Andrews picked up, sounding like he was out of breath.

"Hey, hey," Andrews said, sitting in the chair at his desk.

"Just run a marathon?"

Andrews took a few more seconds to collect his breath. "No, no, I was just on the other side of the office. Wanted to make sure I wasn't in earshot of anyone."

"Oh. Well, I got some news," Recker said. "Not sure if you already know it or not."

"Go ahead."

"Jennings deposited five thousand dollars in a new bank account a few months ago."

"Uh, yeah," Andrews said, shuffling folders around on his desk until he found the right one. He opened it up and started looking at it. "Yeah, it was some consulting work he did on the side or something for some security firm."

"I take it you didn't look too deep into that."

"No, just a cursory look. Everything seemed on the up and up, why?"

"It's a fake company."

"What?" Andrews asked, not believing it.

"There's nothing real about it."

"We ran the basics, everything seemed to come back fine."

"Should've dug deeper," Recker replied.

"Even if that's true, though, that doesn't prove anything."

"It does when you look at the other officers who also opened up false bank accounts with a five-thousand-dollar deposit."

"We didn't find any evidence of that."

"Should've looked harder. One was opened in the name of his wife, the other three in the names of their mothers."

Andrews sighed loudly into the phone, clearly frustrated. "All six got checks from the same security company?"

"You got it."

"Do I need to check this place out?"

"No, don't bother, it'll be a waste of time," Recker answered. "It's a dead end, I've already checked it."

"We still haven't gotten any leads that suggest any of them were anything but clean."

"Well, six officers who are now dead and all opened up bank accounts with a five-thousand-dollar check from a false business sure does raise a lot of red flags, doesn't it?"

"It does. But where do we go from here?"

Recker thought for a few seconds before replying. "Maybe we need to dig into bank accounts for everyone on the force."

Andrews' eyes almost bulged out of his head. "Everyone on the force? You know how long that would take?"

"Plus, wives, spouses, parents, kids, uncles."

"That's a massive undertaking. That'll take months, maybe years, if it can be done at all. You need court orders to check the bank account of everyone on the job."

"You need court orders," Recker said. "I don't play by the same rules, remember."

"But if we're gonna catch the guy behind this, I need solid evidence that I can take into court and put him away with. If they put me on the stand, I very well can't just say The Silencer gave it to me, can I?"

"I suppose not. I'll get back to you when I have more."

"Wait a minute, wait a minute," Andrews said hurriedly.

"What?"

"You have anything else you need me to run down?"

"No, that was it."

"You don't happen to have the bank statements with those deposits, do you?"

"Why?"

"If you do, send them to me, maybe I can use them and talk with their relatives and figure out what's going on. Maybe one of them can tell me something."

Recker didn't reply immediately, but thought it wasn't a bad idea. He wasn't sure how likely it was that one of the cops told anyone in their family what they were doing, especially if it was illegal, but he figured it was probably worth a shot.

"All right, you'll get an email within the hour with what you need."

"Thanks. If any of them say anything interesting, I'll let you know," Andrews said.

The two then hung up, though their conversation gave Recker an idea. He didn't know how workable it was, or how long it would take, but he thought it might just work. But it would depend on Jones' ability. Before telling the others what he was thinking, Recker put his hands in his pocket and paced around the room for a few minutes, trying to get it straight in his own mind. Jones didn't want to wait any longer before finding out what was on his mind, though.

Typing on the keyboard, Jones looked up over his laptop. "Mind sharing what's going through your mind?"

Recker stopped upon hearing his voice, though he didn't hear the entire question. "Huh?"

"You're pacing. Something's going on in that head of yours."

"Oh. Well, I've got an idea."

"Splendid. What is it?"

"Not so sure you'll think it's splendid when I finish saying what it is," Recker said.

"Why is that?"

"Because you'll be doing all the work."

"Oh. If I know you as well as I think I do, I'm going

to say this is going to require quite a bit of computer skill."

"More than me and Chris got for sure."

Jones looked a little beleaguered, knowing his workload was likely going to increase dramatically sometime in the next few minutes. "Might as well just say it."

"I have an idea about how to identify who else might be involved in this."

"Let me stop you right there," Jones said. "Now you're assuming there is someone else involved. Maybe all the work has been done."

"I'm guessing not. I have a feeling the net is gonna catch a lot more fish before this expedition is over."

Jones still looked troubled, but wanted Recker to get on with it. "Well, continue."

"We know six officers got a five-thousand-dollar payment. What if we check into the backgrounds of everyone else to see who else got a five-thousand-dollar payment?"

Jones sat there motionless, batting his eyes for a few moments as he stared at Recker. He couldn't believe what he was saying. "Correct me if I'm wrong, but are you actually suggesting we check into the bank accounts of every single member of the police force?"

Recker made a face as if he'd just been hit with a sharp object, knowing how intensive it sounded. "Yes?"

"Do you know how massive an undertaking that would be?"

"Uh, yes?"

It was one of the few times Jones seemed dumb-founded and at a loss for words. "I, uh, I don't even know where I would start."

"Well you dug up these guys."

"These guys as you put it, I was looking at specifically. Do you know how many officers there are in this city?"

Recker looked at Haley for backup. "What was it at last count, over six thousand? Something like that?"

"I believe so," Haley replied.

"And you want me to check every single one of them?" Jones asked. "And by this question, I'm assuming you don't mean just the officers themselves, but their extended family as well?"

Recker knew how tall a task he was asking and just smiled widely. Jones wasn't ready to give up on telling him just how big it was, though.

"Six thousand officers," Jones said. "Then if you get into spouses, kids, parents, siblings, I mean, the results could be staggering. We could easily reach thirty to forty thousand names before we are done."

Recker tilted his head. "Possible."

Silence filled the room for a minute as Jones thought about how massive a request he was being asked. He had no doubts he could do it, but he knew he couldn't do it quickly. Certainly not fast enough for their purposes. There was just no way it could be done by himself in a fair amount of time. Probably not for months. And that would be with him working basically around the clock and not devoting any time or resources to any of their other cases. It was a thought that didn't hold a lot of value to him.

"I just don't think it would be the best use of our time... my time. Could it be done? Yes. But the time involved," Jones said, shaking his head. "How many other people will not get helped because we've gotten sidetracked on this one issue. A big issue to be sure, no doubt about it, but still... one case as opposed to hundreds of others. And with the evidence starting to point toward criminal circumstances, I'm not sure it's a time investment that's worth making."

Recker listened intently to what Jones was saying and sighed, knowing he was right. The plan could work, but it would just take too long. He nodded in agreement to forget about it. Then Haley snapped his fingers, not ready to let it go so quickly.

"I got it," Haley said.

"What?" Recker asked.

"Something similar. But maybe better. And maybe faster."

Jones was equally intrigued and sat up straighter in his chair to listen. "Well let's hear it."

"Same thing basically, but instead of checking each individual name, we check the bank instead."

Jones' heart sank again, once more realizing how much work that entailed for him. "Do you know how many banks are in the Philadelphia region?"

Haley shrugged, not having any idea. "Gotta be what, a thousand?"

"Maybe two," Recker said.

"That's infinitely better than checking thirty thousand names."

Jones was still not impressed. "Do you know how long and difficult it is to hack into a bank's system?"

Haley threw his hands up to answer the question. Recker, putting some serious thought into it, thought it could really work though. It was much more practical than his previous plan, he thought.

"I've got a better way to make it go more smoothly," Recker said.

Jones didn't seem so convinced. "I would love to hear about it."

"Can you devise a program to only look for certain things in a bank's system?"

"It can be done."

"Every officer's payment has been a flat five thousand dollars. Once you're into the bank's system, have it only look through deposits of exactly five thousand dollars over the past six months. There can't be that many. I mean, how many people will put in a five-thousand-dollar check?"

Jones slouched down a little and leaned back in his chair, putting his index finger on his lips as he thought about it.

Haley tried to make it sound a little easier of a task. "And it's not really even a few thousand banks. Some branches have dozens or a hundred. That'll make it go by a little easier."

Jones looked over at him. "Don't try to sugarcoat it."

"So, what do you think?" Recker asked.

Jones sighed, not really wanting to take on such a task, but reluctantly agreed. "I suppose I can give it a shot. I love how you two make it sound so easy for me."

"Hey, we're willing to help. But like you always say, you got your skills, and we got ours."

"Now you're using my own words against me."

Recker laughed, but then got more serious. "Hey, if it gets to be too much or is more difficult than we thought, then we'll try something else."

"Agreed. I'll do my best. But in the meantime, I'll hope like heck Tyrell finds something before I do. And that's the first time I've ever hoped that someone else found information before me."

"It certainly would make things easier, wouldn't it?"

13

As Jones started hacking his way into different banking institutions, the team still hoped Tyrell would be the one to come up with the missing piece. They all felt like they were close, closer than it appeared they were. Recker thought with the right piece, everything would fall together. Jones figured he could start with the smaller banks and eliminate them a little more quickly, or he could start with the bigger banks, the ones with multiple branches, that way he could eliminate a bunch at one time. He figured it was better to get rid of the most amount possible and started with some of the bigger ones.

Recker was in contact with Tyrell every day, keeping up to date with his progress. Five days had passed since Recker had given him the envelope stuffed with money and he was hoping they'd have a little more to show for it by now. Unfortunately, just as Tyrell had suggested it might go, it seemed to be no different than the first go-round. Nobody seemed to have anything to say. He wasn't through with all his contacts yet, but he wasn't expecting much to change. Tyrell had just left the apartment of one of those contacts when Recker called.

"Yo, what's up?" Tyrell asked.

"Just seeing how you were making out."

"Same as before, man. Whole lotta nothin'."

Recker sighed loudly into the phone to signal his displeasure.

"I feel ya, man, but I don't know what else I can do. I can't make people talk."

"I know," Recker said. "It's not you. I'm just ready to be done with this thing."

"Why you even getting all worked up about it? It's not even your thing, right? I mean, that cop came to you. This ain't on your feet."

"I dunno. Doesn't really matter who came up with it. Fact is, I was asked to help. When I do something, and I can't figure out what's going on or get to the bottom of it, it pisses me off."

"I hear you, man, I hear you."

"Have you talked to everybody again?"

Tyrell took a moment to think and rubbed the back of his head. "Uh, lemme see... uh, no, there's a few more."

"Any chance any of them are promising?"

"Man, I don't wanna even give you the slightest bit of false hope. The chances of one of these cats telling me something is next to nothing."

"All right, I'll talk to you later."

Tyrell kept going, talking to anyone he thought might have had some knowledge of what was going on. One by one, though, he struck out. It'd been several hours since he last spoke to Recker and he thought he should update him on his lack of progress. He pulled his phone out of his pocket and looked at the screen in anticipation of dialing, then just happened to look across the street. He thought he caught a glimpse of a man walking into the neighborhood pharmacy. The man went by the nickname of Bones because he was tall and thin. He had a similar background to Tyrell and was someone who usually knew what was going on in the streets. Tyrell hadn't talked to him previously because Bones had been out of town for the past two weeks. Tyrell crossed the street and ran into the pharmacy to catch up with the man. Once they saw each other, they slapped hands and gave each other a hug.

"Man, where you been keepin' yourself?" Tyrell asked.

"Been spending time with my family over in Jersey for a couple weeks. Going through a rough patch right now?"

"Oh really? What's been going on? Everything all right?"

"Nah, not really. My brother died, and I was over at

his house for a spell, trying to help keep his wife and kids together. It's been rough, man, been real rough."

"Aww, sorry to hear that, bro. They gonna be able to pull through?"

"I dunno. He didn't really have no savings, so it's gonna be hard for them. Gonna be a single woman raising a couple kids. You know how hard that is."

"Yeah."

"I mean, I'll do what I can, send them a few dollars here and there. Just hope I can do enough. It's hard enough making money for my own family, know what I mean?"

"Yeah, definitely do," Tyrell said, hoping they could help each other. "Hey, you think you could help me find some people that I'm looking for?"

"Maybe. Got some names?"

"Man, I got names, pictures, everything."

Tyrell then pulled out the pictures from his new leather jacket and handed them to his friend. Bones took a minute to study them. Tyrell kept a close eye on his friend's face as he looked at the pictures, hoping he'd give off a clue. And he did. Bones made a couple of expressions that showed he might have known them, or at least know something about them. He then passed the pictures back to Tyrell.

Bones shook his head. "Sorry, man, don't know these fellas."

"You sure?"

"Yeah. Can't help you with that."

Tyrell didn't believe him. The clues Bones made with his face told him he did know them. Tyrell moved in closer to him to make sure nobody else in the store could overhear them. "Listen, there could be a lot of money involved in this for you if you know these bulls. All I'm asking is for you to tell me what you know or what they're caught up in. Could really help your family out."

Bones gulped as he nervously looked around the store. Tyrell could see he looked anxious for some reason. He tried to spur Bones on to tell him what he knew.

"Nothing will come back to you. You got my word on that," Tyrell said. "You know I wouldn't put you in a position like that."

"These are some dangerous cats you're playing with, man."

"So, you do know something."

"I know you're messing with some bad people. You'd be best to leave this alone. This is out of your league. Mine too."

"Listen, I'm not asking for me. I'm just working. I've been asked to find the information and pass it along. Whatever happens after this ain't on me or you."

"I dunno, man," Bones said, wiping the sweat off his forehead with the sleeve of his shirt.

Tyrell knew he needed to convince the man a little more. They'd known each other a long time and knew each other's reputations. Like Tyrell, Bones was highly regarded by all who did business with him. He had a reputation of being trustworthy and reliable. Tyrell was about to use that trust.

"Bones, man, this is big. Bigger than the both of us. There's some big-time players involved in this. They're looking for information, and they ain't gonna stop until they get it. Who knows how many people are gonna get hit before this is over?"

"Hit? Whatcha talkin' about?"

Tyrell had forgotten that since Bones was gone for a couple weeks, he probably wasn't as up to speed on what was going on. Tyrell then spent a few minutes explaining the situation.

"So, all those people are dead now?"

"Yeah. You know The Silencer, right?" Tyrell asked.

"Yeah, man, who don't?"

"Well he's in on this."

Bones nodded and took a product off the shelf and went over to the cash register to pay for it. Tyrell walked over to the door and waited for him to finish. After he was done, Bones came over to the door and motioned with his hand for Tyrell to follow him. Bones opened up and started talking as the two walked along the sidewalk.

"How you know The Silencer?" Bones asked.

"Straight up? I do some work for him from time to time."

"Seriously? Wow, that's some shit right there."

"Make sure you keep that on the down low," Tyrell said.

"You ain't gotta worry about that with me, you know that."

"Well, he's looking for these guys. He knows something's going on. And believe me, he ain't gonna stop looking."

Bones seemed to be more willing to talk about the subject knowing Recker was in on it, though he appeared to be more interested in finding out more about The Silencer. "What kind of guy is he, man? What's he like?"

"Who? The Silencer?"

"Yeah."

"He's a good dude, man. A really good dude. Got good intentions, wants to do right by people. It don't matter if you're black, white, Asian, catholic, protestant, Muslim, he don't care about none of that. To him, you're either good or bad."

Bones let out a laugh. "What's he working with you for then? You know, me and you, we're not exactly classified as great citizens."

"Nah, it's not like that with him. He's after the real bad dudes. He's not after guys like you and me just trying to survive. We don't really hurt nobody. He's after the people who got black hearts, who don't give a crap about who they hurt as long as they benefit from it."

Tyrell could tell Bones was still wrestling with

whether he should tell what he knew. Though he thought his friend would eventually get there, Tyrell figured he'd sweeten the pot to get there sooner. He pulled out the white envelope from his pocket and waved it in front of him, making sure Bones saw it.

"There's three thousand in here," Tyrell said. "He authorized me to give it to whoever gave me the information he's looking for."

"Three thousand?"

"Yeah, as long as the information checks out. Think about it, man. That's three thousand you could give to your brother's family, help them out. Do some good by them. You ain't mixed up in any of this, are you?"

"Nah, it's not like that. I just don't want it to get back to me."

"You got my word on that, bro. I don't need to tell anyone where the info came from."

Bones stared at the envelope, enticed by what was inside. "When would I get that?"

"Probably a day or two. I'll relay the information, he'll check it out. If everything comes back good, I'll swing by you and hand it off."

"Then that's it?"

"That's the end of it."

Bones nodded, agreeing to the terms of the deal. They stopped walking and scurried over against the wall of the storefront they were in front of. Bones took another look around just to make sure nobody was nearby listening.

"OK, I don't know all the details of what's going on and all."

"Just tell me what you know," Tyrell said.

"All right. I don't know all the people in those pictures you showed me. But I recognized two of them."

Tyrell quickly dug the photos out of his jacket and showed them again, so Bones could point them out. "Which ones?"

Bones pointed to the two that he knew, then Tyrell shoved them back in his pocket.

"You know those guys were cops, right?" Tyrell asked.

"Yeah. There's a few more of them too."

"There are? You know their names?"

Bones made a face and shook his head. "Nah, not their real names. Know a few nicknames though if that helps."

"Yeah, that'll help a lot."

"The other two guys I know, one guy is nicknamed Siv, the other was nicknamed Butch."

"Siv and Butch?" Tyrell asked. "They variations of their names or something?"

Bones shrugged. "No idea, man. Just know that's what they were called."

"You actually seen this Siv and Butch?"

"Yeah, a couple times. They're cops too from what I understand."

"You know what all this stuff's about?"

"I can't say for sure about the shootings or anything like that," Bones answered. "But the two I pointed out, and the two names I gave you, they were dealing. They were into some heavy stuff."

"The cops were dealing?"

"Yeah. It goes like this. Ever since Jeremiah got taken out, everything in this town goes through Vincent. At least the main stuff. There's some little dealers here and there that either Vincent don't know about or he just don't care because they ain't that big yet. I mean, you know all this, I ain't gotta tell you that."

"What about these guys?"

"They see an opportunity to pick up where Jeremiah fell. They think they can make a lot of bread and Vincent won't be able to touch them because they're cops. Either that or they'll make a deal with Vincent where they'll scratch each other's backs or something."

Tyrell thought it sounded good, but there were still a few things that didn't make sense to him. "So, who's killing these guys then? Is it Vincent? He knows there's a new group coming up, and he's putting them down. Or are the cops taking out their own? Fighting with each other or something?"

Bones shrugged, not having any idea. "I don't know. What I do know, is these guys were starting to make some deals, make contacts, putting stuff together. All the other stuff that's been going on, I can't speak to that."

Tyrell nodded, taking it all in. Once they were finished, and Bones gave him all the information he had, Tyrell handed him the envelope. Bones looked a little surprised that he was giving it to him already.

"What's this?" Bones asked. "I thought you had to check out what I was saying first."

"I believe you. I don't think you'd make all that up."

"Never know, man. I could be lying to you."

Tyrell smiled. "Hey, it's no skin off my nose. Don't mean nothin' to me. The Silencer, though? That's another story. Trust me, if you're lying, he will find you."

"I got nothing to worry about. It'll check out."

"I know it will."

"Hey, are you like, real tight with him?" Bones asked.

"Why?"

"I dunno. You said you do some work for him from time to time."

"Yeah."

"Maybe you could put in a word for me if he ever needs something. You know, look me up. You know I know things out here. Maybe I could help him out if the price is right."

The two men shook hands as they finished their talk. "I'll put the word in."

14

After Tyrell was done with his questioning, he went back to his house before calling Recker to let him know what he found out. Though he did trust what Bones had told him, Tyrell liked being extra cautious whenever he found out interesting information. He didn't like to blab about it in public places, just in case there were wandering ears around. Plus, if someone was watching or following him, he didn't want to make it seem like he got something so good he had to call someone about it right away. That would immediately make Bones look bad and put him in danger if those cops happened to be watching him. Tyrell just didn't take those kinds of chances. He wanted to make it look like they were just having a normal conversation between friends.

Once Tyrell did call Recker, he recalled his entire conversation with Bones, not leaving any details out.

He even went over it two times to make sure he didn't forget anything. Recker was happy they finally had a lead to work on, though he still had questions and reservations about it. He was taking information from someone he didn't know. He always was hesitant to do that, even though he trusted Tyrell's judgment completely.

"How solid do you think this information is?" Recker asked.

"I think it's good. Real good."

"You trust this guy?"

"I do. I think he was straight up leveling. I don't have any doubts about that."

"All right. Good job with everything."

"Thank you, thank you. Just my normal excellent work," Tyrell said with a laugh.

"OK, we'll take it from here."

"You got it. You need something else, just let me know."

"We will."

After hanging up, Recker then let Jones know what Tyrell found out. Haley was working on a case and wasn't scheduled to be back until later that night. Before doing anything, they discussed it amongst each other for a few minutes.

"What do you think? Call Detective Andrews and give him the names?" Jones asked.

Recker shook his head. "No, I don't think so. I don't

think we should tell anyone about this until we're certain what's going on."

"Well, let's find out who this Siv and Butch are first."

Jones immediately went to work on his computer, pulling up police personnel files. He typed in the names to see if anything popped up automatically, not that he was expecting it to. They didn't sound like last names to him. Nothing came up instantly. Recker pulled up a chair next to him and started looking through the files on another computer, seeing if any names looked similar. He was quickly halted by Jones, who had started another search already.

"Hold on, hold on," Jones said, tapping Recker on the shoulder.

"What's up? Find something?"

"Possibly."

With Jones' first search, he was looking for those two names specifically. He then performed a search for any names that included Siv or Butch, even a partial name. He got a hit on one of them.

"There's a few possibles," Jones said, reading the screen, then pointing to some names. "Here, you take these three, see if there's any connection to our list of fallen officers. I'll take the other three."

After both men looked at their respective lists, Recker couldn't see any connection to the officers who were killed. Jones, though, thought he found the missing link.

"I've got it," Jones said. "Detective Jay Sivelski."

Recker eagerly moved his chair over to see the screen and started to read it. "He knew Jennings."

"Indeed, he did. It appears he also knew Bridges. I can link him to those two. He recently worked cases involving both officers."

They spent a few more hours trying to learn the identity of the man they knew as Butch. But it was to no avail. They couldn't find any evidence of someone named Butch. But it didn't mean he wasn't there. They knew he had to be. Once they found the first name, they knew the other one wasn't far behind. After exhaustively searching, both Recker and Jones leaned back in their chairs to decide their next move in finding out the man's real name.

"I think we should contact Andrews," Jones said.

Recker looked at him, not sure he wanted to go in that direction yet. "I dunno. If they're guys he knows, friends with, it might complicate things."

"But won't it eventually get to that point, anyway? I mean, what difference does it make if you talk to him about it now or you wait a week or two until we have all the evidence and lay it out for him? The circumstances will still be the same."

Recker nodded. "Yeah, I guess you're right about that."

"And whatever happens as a result of it, we will get there sooner. Besides, aren't you the one who said we should trust him?"

"Don't go using my own words against me."

Recker concluded that calling Andrews was the right move. Hopefully, he could figure out who the other guy they were looking for was. The detective didn't pick up until after the fifth ring.

"Hope this isn't a bad time," Recker said.

"Uh, no, no. I was just at home. Had the phone in a different room."

"Day off?"

"Yeah. Yeah, I get them occasionally."

"Must be nice."

"So, what can I do for you?" Andrews asked.

"I'm getting closer to figuring out what this is all about. I need your help to connect some missing pieces though."

"OK. What do you need?"

"First of all, you're probably not gonna like some of what I've learned. I need to know whether I should push on with this or just cut bait now."

"Why? What's the difference?"

"Well, if you're on board with what I tell you, then I can proceed," Recker said. "But if you're one of those cops who doesn't want to bring any dirt on fellow cops, then I'm wasting my time and I'm not gonna want to go any further."

Andrews already knew what that meant without having to be told. "They're dirty, aren't they?"

"Yeah. Yeah, they are."

"What difference does my opinion make to you? Wouldn't you do the same thing, regardless?"

"No. I'm not waging a war against cops, dirty or not," Recker answered. "I know some in the department have a high opinion of me. Maybe that gets me extra leeway in terms of people looking for me, maybe not, I don't know. But I do know I'm not jeopardizing that reputation over something that may get swept under the rug, anyway. Only time I would go after a cop is if an innocent person's life was at stake. Cops engaged in criminal activities with other criminals isn't something that really bothers me to be honest."

"OK. I hear what you're saying. And I'm on board. I'm not a saint. You know I've done things for Vincent. But cops are being killed out there. And if other cops did it, then that's something that we need to do something about. Everyone in the department will be on board for that. So, whatever you got, just lay it out there."

"OK. I've got two names for you. Do you know a Detective Jay Sivelski?"

Andrews thought for a second, but that was all he needed. "Uh, yeah, Sivelski? Yeah, I know Siv."

"Well he's involved. There's another name, but it's only a nickname, that's all I've got."

"What is it?"

"Guy's name is Butch."

"Butch. Butch," Andrews said, taking a minute to think about it.

"Anything?"

"Uh, yeah, maybe. There's a guy in patrol, Barry Orwell, he's a sergeant, his nickname is Butch."

"You know him?" Recker asked.

"I mean, I've bumped into him a few times, but I don't know him that well or anything."

"But you know Sivelski?"

"Yeah, I've worked with him a few times. How are these guys involved?"

"That I don't know," Recker said. "I don't know if they're gonna wind up like the others, or whether they're at the top of the food chain, but I know one thing, somebody's gotta be running this thing."

"Well if you're looking for leaders, Siv would be at the top of my list."

"Why's that?"

"He's a go-getter," Andrews said. "He's a take charge kind of guy. Orwell too. Big, muscular type of guy. Doesn't mind giving orders. Wouldn't be surprised if they were the ones giving directions."

"Well, we need to find out who else is in their little group, exactly what they got going on, and why some of them are getting knocked off."

Before finishing their conversation, Recker agreed to send Andrews via email some of the things they'd uncovered. After putting his phone away, Recker sat on the desk with his back to Jones and looked out the window. Something still didn't seem right to him.

"What is it now?" Jones asked.

"What?"

"What else are you concerned about?"

"Something doesn't feel right," Recker answered.

"How so?"

"We're now going by the assumption that for some reason these cops are knocking each other off, right?"

"Yes, I suppose so."

"That's what's bothering me," Recker said.

"What? You don't think they would turn on each other? They're as much criminals as they are police officers. That's what criminals do."

"Yeah, but I dunno, it's just... it's not making sense to me. If you're gonna knock off fellow cops that have been in your little group that've been doing not so nice things, then that means you either don't trust them, or they're making a lot of mistakes."

"Or perhaps they changed their mind and don't want to continue those pursuits," Jones said.

"Maybe. But that still baffles me. If I'm a cop and I wanna do something like this, don't you think I would make damn sure that whoever I pick to join me, is in it for life? That in six months or a year they're not gonna change their mind and put everything I was working for in jeopardy? I'm having a tough time wrapping my head around that."

Jones nodded. "I see what you mean. Perhaps you're right about that. Maybe they are not picking themselves off."

"If that's the case, then we're back to where we

started. If it's not them, then cops are getting killed and we don't still don't know by who."

Jones put his index finger in the air to counter the point. "Not necessarily. Whichever way it leans, we're still closer than we were in the beginning. We now have a pretty good idea why this is happening. We just need to narrow it down a bit further."

Recker got off the desk and started walking around the room, still deep in thought. If they went with the theory that the police officers weren't killing their own, which was viable conjecture, then they had to figure out who would have wanted them dead. And he kept coming back to the same conclusion, even if he didn't want it to be so. He went back to the desk and sat next to Jones as he sought confirmation of his opinion.

"So, if it seems unlikely that the cops are killing each other, and I'm not saying that it is yet, who would stand to benefit by that?"

Jones' eyes danced around the room as he thought about it, though he was unable to come up with an answer. "I don't know."

"Think about it. There's one major criminal organization in town and we both know who runs it."

"Vincent."

"He told me himself he doesn't worry about small players," Recker said. "That he doesn't worry about anyone until they start trying to grow bigger."

"And you think he may have viewed this upstart crew as a threat?"

"He said he didn't know anything about this crew. We know they've been in operation for at least six months, and probably up to a year. You think Vincent would be in the dark about a bunch of rogue cops going into business for themselves? In territory that he supposedly owns?"

"It does seem somewhat peculiar that he would not know," Jones answered.

"And, considering he's got cops on his payroll, don't you think one or two of them may have gotten wind about something like that and let him know what was going on? Even if they didn't know exact specifics. Even if they only had suspicions of something or heard whispers that someone was looking to take a percentage of his operation. Don't you think they would've told him about it?"

"It does seem likely. But then again, he came to you to help investigate this matter. Why would he do that if he was involved? Surely, he knew you would eventually get to the bottom of it and figure out the details. He knows you well enough by now to know you would. But even if he only knew you by reputation, it would seem like a gamble that doesn't need to be taken. He's smarter than that."

"Unless he figured that I'd somehow get swept up in it anyway and tried to manipulate how things went from the beginning of it."

"I'm not sure I can picture Vincent killing cops, regardless of whether they were involved in illegal activities or branching out and taking a piece of his profits."

"Well, I don't think it's something he'd prefer to do if there were other options available," Recker said. "But maybe he didn't think there were other options."

15

Three days after the investigation into Detective Sivelski and Sergeant Orwell began, another police officer was killed. Unlike the others, it didn't take long for Recker and Jones to link this one together. This time, they connected the officer to Orwell and Wheaton immediately, and also found a five-thousand-dollar bank deposit in the officer's name. Recker was beginning to get impatient as he sought to conclude the case. When he started this endeavor with Jones, he swore he'd never get between criminals who were looking to knock each other off. And now, it seemed as if that's what he was doing.

Though the victims were cops, they were obviously into some bad stuff, and whoever was knocking them off, Recker wasn't sure if he should be getting involved in it. That's why he came up with the idea to get right to the heart of the matter. Jones thought it was very risky and something they didn't need to chance right then. But as usual, Recker won out.

Recker and Haley were waiting inside the home of Detective Sivelski. It was a little after eleven, and his wife and kids were upstairs sleeping. They'd only been waiting for about twenty minutes. They had Tyrell watching the district Sivelski was working out of and let them know when he left to go home. Detective Andrews had told Recker what shifts Sivelski was working so they could coordinate the best time to talk with him.

Recker was waiting in the living room, off to the side of the house. Haley was stationed near the back door. When the headlights from the driveway flashed through the windows, they knew the detective was home. With the living room pitch black, Sivelski wouldn't see Recker until it was too late. Within a few minutes, the door started wiggling with the sound of clanging keys just outside it. Recker was sitting on a chair in the corner of the room, waiting for a light to turn on. Once the door closed, Sivelski walked over to a lamp and turned it on. He immediately jumped back when he saw the strange man sitting in his living room. He reached for his gun inside his jacket.

"I wouldn't do that," Recker said.

Sivelski, noticing how calm the man was, and that he didn't have a gun in his hands, stopped his movements. "What do you want?"

"Just to chat."

"Who are you?" Sivelski asked. He then looked at the stairs, thinking of his wife and children.

"They're fine. Sleeping. I'm not here to hurt anybody."

"Then what do you want?"

"Answers."

"To what?"

"Sit down," Recker said. "And before you get any sparkling ideas of doing anything other than exactly what I say, know there's another man in the next room over."

"You're bluffing."

Recker smiled. "I don't bluff. Ever."

By the serious look on the man's face, Sivelski took him at his word and sat. "So, what's this about?"

"I know the things you've been doing outside your police duties."

Sivelski put a strange look on his face and shrugged, pretending to have no idea what was being referred to. Recker knew that pulling the truth out of the detective's mouth wasn't going to be easy, so he looked to speed the process up. He reached into his pocket and pulled out a bunch of folded up pieces of paper. He then just tossed the papers onto the floor, one by one.

"Bank statements for you and your buddies," Recker said. "Including the five-thousand-dollar deposits. The fake security company you set up to try to disguise it. Statements from people who say you're trying to move into Vincent's territory. How long do you wanna try to keep up this charade?"

"What's it to you?"

"People have asked me to look into it."

Sivelski scrunched his eyebrows together as he looked at the man more closely. After scrutinizing him further, he recognized the face, and a wry smile developed across his lips. "Ah, I know you who are now. You're the city savior, the crusader that's helping little old ladies cross the street and saving cats stuck up in trees."

Recker took no offense to his obvious insult. Instead of getting angry, he replied with his usual sense of humor. "I don't know where you get your information, but I haven't saved any cats in trees."

"My mistake."

"I take it you're not one of my biggest fans."

"I can take you or leave you, man. Are you expecting me to confess to something? Kill me? What's your play here?"

Recker shook his head. "There's no play. And if I wanted you dead, you would be already. I just want to have an honest conversation with you and then I'll be on my way."

"Then I'm on my way to jail, is that it?" Sivelski asked.

"Listen, I'm not really interested in seeing you go anywhere."

"Then what are you doing here?"

"I'll be honest with you if you agree to do the same."

Sivelski shrugged, waiting to see what he had to say first. "We'll see."

"A member of your department reached out to a mutual contact of ours to see if I'd look in on the case."

"Why would they do that?"

"Apparently, they had no leads," Recker said. "I guess when cops start going down and there are no suspects, you tend to get desperate and look for help in unorthodox places."

"And you think that leads to me?"

"Unless you're telling me you're not responsible for it."

"I don't really need to tell you anything."

Recker was starting to get aggravated at the lack of cooperation. "Listen, I don't really wanna play this game with you all night. I've got other things to do and I wanna move on from this case. If you are involved in killing other cops, then it doesn't really concern me. If it's someone else, then I'd like to find out who it is."

Sivelski moved his head around as he thought of what to do. "You really think I would have killed other cops?"

"I have no idea."

"And if I admit to anything here? What then?"

Recker could sense the man's wall was starting to

break down. "Whatever's said here stays between you and me."

Sivelski rubbed his mouth and nose before replying. "All right. Honestly, I had nothing to do with those guys being killed. I have no reason to do that."

"So you guys were starting your own little operation on the side?"

Sivelski hesitated before answering. "Yes. There's a lot of money to be made out there. We sure ain't gonna get rich being on the job. Why not? There's not a lot of competition out there."

"Except for Vincent."

"We figured we could handle him. Besides, he'd have to be crazy to think he could take us on."

"Have you butted heads with him yet?" Recker asked.

"Yeah, we've had some words."

"He definitely knows about you guys?"

"Oh, yeah. I talked to him myself."

"I talked to him a few days ago. He said he didn't know anything about you guys."

Sivelski made a displeased face. "He's lying out his ass."

"Do you have any idea who's been killing these guys?"

Sivelski shook his head and shrugged. "If I did, don't you think I'd have taken care of it already?"

"Not necessarily. It'd be hard for you to do that and explain how you know that. I would think you'd have

to explain how your relationship with those other officers works."

"Really not as difficult as you make it sound."

"You think it's Vincent taking you guys out?"
Recker asked.

"I don't know. Maybe. I don't know if he's dumb
enough to do that though. He'd know how much heat
that'd bring down on him."

"Who's in charge of this operation? You? Or
Butch?"

Sivelski looked surprised that he knew the
sergeant's name.

"Yeah, I know."

"It's my deal. They all take orders from me."

"So how many more you got on this gig?" Recker
asked. He could see that Sivelski was hesitant in
answering the question by how he was shifting in his
seat and stalling. "Might as well tell me. I'm gonna find
out on my own anyway."

"Three more."

"Any of you worried about being the next one with
a hollow-point bullet buried inside you?"

"We're working on it."

"Hope you make it fast or else this case will be over
for me before we know it."

"I'm touched by your caring philosophy about our
well-being," Sivelski said.

"Well, before any more of you wind up in the cemetery, maybe you should try to put out the word to save yourselves."

"The word? What word?"

"That you're leaving the business. You obviously stepped on the wrong toes of somebody," Recker answered. "And they're letting you know it. One dead body at a time. If you don't let them know quickly, that wife of yours upstairs is gonna be planning your funeral."

"I'll keep that in mind."

Recker was satisfied with the question-and-answer session and believed he was getting the truth out of the detective. He didn't have anything else that needed to be said. He got up and walked across the room to the front door. Just as he opened it, he turned back to look at the detective, who was still sitting in the same spot. "Maybe you should stick with what you're supposed to do best. Protecting the people out there."

Recker didn't wait for a response before leaving and just walked out the door. But there wasn't one coming, anyway. Sivelski had nothing else to say. All he could do from that point was think about their discussion and figure out what he wanted to do from there. After leaving the house, Recker let Haley know he was gone so he could slip out the back. They both walked around the block to get back to their car, getting there at the same time.

"Get what you wanted?" Haley asked.

"Yeah, I think so."

They went straight back to the office so Haley could pick up his car as both went home for the night after that. Along with Jones, they'd already agreed that whatever was learned, they'd reconvene in the morning to go over it, as well as discuss their next options moving forward.

Feeling like they were at the cusp of figuring the entire plot out, Recker got to the office earlier than normal the next morning to get a jump on things. As usual, Jones had already beaten him to the punch.

"How long you been going at it?" Recker asked.

"Oh, about since six."

"Heard from Chris yet?"

"Yes, he just texted me a few minutes ago," Jones said. "He's picking up breakfast on the way in. Should be here in a half hour or so."

"Good. We have a lot to discuss."

Recker then told Jones about his conversation with Sivelski, letting him know everything that was said, as well as his own suspicions. After he was finished, Jones had a hard time believing it.

"You really believe Vincent is behind this?"

Recker nodded. "I do. No one else could pull this off. No one else would have the stones to do this."

"But why?"

"I think he got wind of a growing threat and put an end to it quickly."

"But why play the game like he has no idea what's going on?" Jones asked.

"I've been thinking about that. Put yourself in his shoes. If it gets out that he's the one behind the killings, how much heat will that bring him?"

"A considerable amount."

"More than he wants. He's not stupid. He's got cops on his payroll. If they find out that he's taking out cops, even ones that are dirty, who's to say whether they'll turn on him? Even the dirty ones tend to stick together. But just the same, he wants to take out anyone who's competing against him. Just makes it trickier when they're wearing badges."

"Makes it trickier to determine what we should do too," Jones said.

"From what I can tell, we have a couple options."

"Which are?"

"We forget about this entire thing and let whatever happens happen. Or we barrel into it head on and go wherever it takes us."

"Meaning we take on Vincent."

"And probably throw away all the goodwill we've built up with him along the way in the process," Recker said.

"Or? Maybe we tell him what we know and see if he comes clean."

Recker didn't think that was a wise idea though. "No. That would just put us on a collision course again. But there is another solution."

"And that is?"

"That Sivelski and his bunch admit that they're in

over their heads and admit defeat."

"And just how likely do you think that is?" Jones asked.

"I guess that depends."

"On what?"

"On how much they want to live."

Recker asked for an emergency meeting with Vincent based on his conversation with Detective Sivelski. He didn't let the crime boss know what the meeting was about in advance. Luckily, based on their past relationship, Vincent always made time for him. Since it was mid-afternoon, Vincent told him to meet him at his trucking business where they'd conducted so many meetings before. Once Recker arrived, Malloy led him to the same office as usual. Like usual, Vincent was sitting behind his desk as Recker walked in. He took a seat, not wanting to waste any time on the subject.

"So, what's this about?" Vincent asked. "Seemed pretty urgent based on your call."

"I would just like to know from you where things stand."

"From me? In regard to?"

"This whole cop thing," Recker answered.

"I thought we'd been over that."

"And I talked to a certain detective who's involved in a group of cops who started going into business for themselves who told me that you've talked to them about their business."

Vincent stared at Recker for a few moments, taken slightly off guard. But he remained cool and calm like he usually did. "If you're referring to a Detective Sivelski, then yes, I know all about him and his little operation."

"You told me before you didn't."

"You showed me pictures and names of men who'd been killed. You asked me if I knew them. I did not."

"So, you didn't know they were part of Sivelski's crew?"

"I did not."

"You know how it looks, right?" Recker asked. "You told me yourself that you don't pay attention to people until they start getting bigger. Then suddenly, this crew, who looks like they could be a threat due to their positions, and they start dropping like flies."

Vincent grinned, knowing how it appeared, but not ready to admit any involvement. "I can see how it might look to some. I can't really help outside appearances though, can I?"

"So, you're saying that you're not responsible for taking these people out?"

Vincent leaned forward and put his hands on the desk. "Even if I said I did have a hand in it, and to be clear, I'm not saying I did, where would that put us?"

Recker shrugged. "Same place as before. I don't think it would change our deal at all. I'm just looking for answers."

Vincent smiled again. "Well that's good to know.

But in saying that, my answer still hasn't changed. Whatever is happening to these officers is not my doing."

Recker nodded, feeling like they didn't have much else to discuss. He still couldn't be sure whether Vincent was actually being truthful with him, but even if he wasn't, it was obvious that he wasn't going to admit to anything. Before he left, though, Vincent had some parting words for him.

"I'll tell you, Mike, since this is starting to look like I have a hand in it, that's very concerning to me. Makes me look guilty."

"So?"

"So, I'm going to start putting my people on it."

"To do what?"

"To find who *is* responsible for this. Jimmy," Vincent said, pointing toward the door. "Start making the arrangements."

"You got it, boss," Malloy replied.

Recker looked at him, not sure of his motives. But whatever they were, hopefully it would help resolve the situation sooner.

"I guarantee you that we'll find this person by the end of the week," Vincent said.

Recker went back to the office to talk to Jones and Haley about the meeting. Though he was initially convinced Vincent was the mastermind behind what was going on, now, he just wasn't sure. Jones and Haley were equally as perplexed. They had their theories, several different versions of them, and they all made sense, but they couldn't prove any of them. Not yet. And they weren't sure they could. Unless more bodies dropped.

16

Recker was having another conversation with Vincent. This time it was on the phone, even though it wasn't Vincent's preferred method of contact. Recker was pacing around the office as he talked, with Jones and Haley working on computers, though both were keeping an ear out to try to get some inclination of what they were discussing. Even if they couldn't hear any specifics, they had a good idea of what was being talked about.

It'd been five days since Recker's emergency meeting with Vincent. In that time, Recker tasked Tyrell with keeping an ear out on the street to see if he got wind of Sivelski throwing in the white towel. Tyrell reported back after a couple of days that he heard no such development. And they'd soon learn the consequences of that. Two days ago, news broke out Sergeant Barry Orwell had been killed on duty after responding to what was supposed to be a domestic disturbance. But when he arrived at the house in question, there was no disturbance. In walking back to his car, a shot rang out across the street, killing him instantly.

Last night, they were greeted with the news Detective Sivelski had been murdered, only a few steps from his front door. Recker and company were reasonably confident that was the last of the police shootings. Though there were three other members of the police crew still at large, they weren't the brains of the outfit. With the two leaders, Sivelski and Orwell, being killed, it was believed the others would cease operations. But it still left questions unanswered, such as, who was behind it. Most people didn't know the reasonings behind the killings, and for them, it was still an uncomfortable time. For all they knew, some nut job was targeting police officers. Most people would still need closure. That's basically all Recker was still looking for to provide.

Once Recker got off the phone, he kept walking around the office for a minute. Eventually, he came back over to the desk and tossed his phone on it. He stood there, not saying a word, leaning on the desk. Both Jones and Haley looked up at him, and both read him the same way. He didn't look particularly pleased.

"Would you care to tell us what that look on your face is for?" Jones asked.

"He says they're close."

"Close to what?"

"Finding the person responsible," Recker answered.

"Well that's good news."

"Yeah, so why don't you look happy about it?" Haley asked.

"I dunno. I guess because I just find it hard to believe."

"Why?" Jones said. "You know Vincent has plenty of contacts on the street, more than we do. What's hard to believe about it?"

"Just doesn't feel right. This whole thing hasn't felt right for a while."

"Well, regardless of that, it seems as though it might be coming to a head. And that's what we want, isn't it?"

"I guess so."

"I'll be glad when it is," Jones said. "I'm ready to put all of this behind us. You know I wasn't exactly thrilled about taking this case on to start with. I'll be happy to not have to put any more time and resources into it."

"Do we even need to keep looking into it?" Haley asked. "I mean, if Vincent's close, then it seems like he's further ahead of things than we are right now. Maybe we shouldn't even bother checking anymore."

Recker wasn't too keen on that idea. "Well, let's keep on it a few more days, just in case Vincent isn't as close as he thinks he is."

Jones was only too happy to oblige Haley's suggestion and started shifting some of his time to other things, though he still kept an eye on things. But from his vantage point, there wasn't much else he could do. It seemed as though all the computer work that was necessary had already been done. While Jones started looking into other upcoming cases, Recker and Haley stayed on their current assignments. They were still working on those assignments when Tyrell called about six hours later.

"What's up, Tyrell?"

"Hey, got something big for you."

"What is it?"

"Might have a name for you," Tyrell said.

"Name of who?"

"Of the guy who's been shooting cops."

"What?" Recker said, almost in complete disbelief.

"I think I got the guy."

"What's his name?"

"Jeffrey Flowers."

Recker snapped his fingers to get his partner's attention. Once he did, he repeated the name to them, so they could start digging up his background information.

"How'd you get this?" Recker asked.

"Well you said to keep digging, keep pressing. That's what I've been doing."

As was his nature, Recker was still skeptical. "And

someone just finally came to you and volunteered the information?"

"I dunno, man. I've just been continuing to work it."

"The guy who told you, you know him?"

"Yeah, I've dealt with him a time or two over the years."

"You trust him?"

"Yeah, you know, as much as you trust anybody out here," Tyrell answered.

"What's your take on it?"

"I think it's good."

"All right, we'll start checking it out," Recker said.

"It is kind of strange now that I think about it."

"What's that?"

"Well, this dude does a lot of work for Vincent. Even more than I have. Kind of weird that he'd come to me with the info instead of just giving it to him."

"Vincent told me he was getting close. Maybe this is what he meant."

"No, I don't think so."

"Why not?" Recker asked.

"Because he told me he didn't mention it to him."

"How much did you have to give him for it?"

"Only five hundred," Tyrell said.

"Five hundred? That's it?"

"That's it."

"A tip like that is worth a ton more than that. Why would he just give it to you for such a low amount?"

"Beats me. People out here do some strange things from time to time. Can't always figure out someone's motivations."

"I'll go along with that."

As soon as Recker was done on the phone, he checked out the computer to see what Jones had on Flowers. As they ran down his list of prior criminal offenses, the red flags in Recker's mind were going off. It didn't seem to match up with the type of person he was expecting to be behind the killings.

"There's nothing on there that indicates he's the guy we're looking for," Recker said. "I mean, there's not a violent crime on there."

"That does not mean he hasn't upped his game," Jones said.

"David."

"I know it does not seem likely. But nevertheless, it needs to be checked out, does it not?"

"Yeah."

"Well then, let's see if I can pin down an address for him and investigate. Then we can come up with our own conclusion."

"Kind of funny, guy with the last name of Flowers doing stuff like this," Haley said, appreciating the irony.

"Yeah. A lot of funny things seem to be going on here," Recker replied.

"Besides his history, what else is bothering you about him?" Jones asked. "Or is that it?"

"A guy who's known to associate with Vincent, one of his contacts on the street, and he doesn't go straight to him with it? Instead, he comes to us? And for only five hundred dollars? That just screams all kinds of nonsense to me."

"As I said, let's just check it out and see what comes of it."

Recker agreed, and even if he thought it was a false lead, it was still a lead that needed to be run down. Jones spent roughly thirty minutes on the computer before he came up with something. He printed it out and handed it to Recker.

"Lives in an apartment off the boulevard," Jones said.

Recker looked at the time and figured it was best to wait another hour or two for darkness to really set in before heading over there. He went over to his cabinet and pulled out a couple weapons for his next rendezvous, then looked at Haley.

"Feel like having some fun tonight?"

"I think I could be persuaded to join the party," Haley replied.

"Please, just exercise some caution when you get there," Jones said. "I realize he doesn't have a violent past on paper, but that doesn't mean he hasn't graduated, or that he isn't dangerous."

"Don't worry. I won't be taking anyone for granted on this case," Recker said.

Once ten o'clock rolled around, Recker and Haley left the office on the way to Flowers' apartment. It was a modest apartment in a decent area, not some run-down place off the grid or an apartment people tried to hide out in. They staked it out for an hour or so, trying to work out if he was there or not. Flowers had an apartment with a balcony on the third floor, so Haley waited by the outside, looking up at it, waiting for signs of movement. It was dark the entire time they were there, leading them to believe the man they were looking for may not have been home.

Recker didn't want to wait any longer and went up to the third floor and stood outside Flowers' apartment. He stationed himself there for a few minutes, keeping his ear pressed to the door as he struggled to hear any type of noise coming from inside. After five more minutes of inactivity, believing the apartment was empty, Recker let Haley know he was going in. Haley moved from the back of the apartment to join his friend inside.

Recker picked the lock and opened the door. He had his gun out, ready for a battle if one presented itself. It was dark and not a single sound was heard. Hesitant to go any further for fear something was waiting for him, he put his hand on the wall to feel for a light switch. After a few seconds of searching, he found it and flicked it on. As soon as the lights went on, Recker's eyes were immediately drawn to the middle of the floor in the living room area. There was a man's body, lying face down. Blood was starting to seep out from the outline of his body and staining the carpet.

"We got one down," Recker said.

"There in thirty," Haley replied.

Recker started checking the other rooms. There were two bedrooms, a bathroom, and a kitchen. He cleared the kitchen first before starting on the others. He stepped over the dead body as he walked to the other rooms. As he was in the first bedroom, Haley announced his presence to make sure Recker knew it was him if he heard noises.

"I'm in," Haley said, closing the door behind him so nobody could sneak up on him.

"Check the bedroom on the left. I got the other one and the bathroom."

"Got it."

After the two searched the other rooms, the place was empty. They met back up in the living room to go over the situation. Recker knelt beside the body to get a better look at his face.

"That Flowers?" Haley asked.

"Yep. Spitting image. Looks just like his picture."

"What do you think happened?"

"I dunno," Recker said, pushing the body off the floor just enough to see the blood coming out of two holes in his chest. "I'd say from the amount of blood he's lost that he got shot."

Haley looked around the room, noticing two shell casings on the floor and pointed them out. "There's the evidence."

Recker stood and looked around the room. He then started searching through it as Haley looked through the bedrooms. They were looking for anything that would tie him to the case. It didn't take long for them to find it.

"In here," Haley shouted.

Recker quickly came in, seeing Haley rummage around through a dresser drawer.

"Whatcha got?" Recker asked.

Haley was careful not to touch anything with his hands so as not to leave fingerprints and used a shirt to pick up the evidence.

"Gun," he said, picking it up and holding it high for his partner to see. He then set it back down in the drawer and picked up a box. "Ammunition."

"Hollow-point bullets," Recker said.

By the look on Recker's face, Haley could see he still didn't look pleased.

"Hoping this stuff wouldn't be there?" Haley asked.

"I dunno. Maybe. Just seems like everything's been tied up neatly."

"Well, I think our work here is done. Should probably get out of here soon before the police come. Someone might have called them already."

"Yeah. Let's go," Recker said.

They left the apartment and called Jones to let him know Flowers was dead, and not of their doing. It was a good thing they decided to leave when they did, or they would have had to deal with a police presence, as they showed up only five minutes later. They agreed to go home for the night and meet up again in the morning to go over their next steps. Recker was the last one to arrive in the office the following morning.

"Everyone see this?" Recker asked, tossing the newspaper down on the desk, which indicated the cop killer had been killed himself.

"Yes," Jones said.

"Seems as though it's wrapped up."

"So why do you still sound unhappy?"

Recker shook his head and sighed. "Because it all just seems so neat and tidy. I mean, c'mon, you guys don't really think Flowers did this, do you?"

"Even if he was set up to be the patsy, there's not much else we can do at this point," Haley replied. "He's been made to look guilty, the rest of the crew is going to scatter, there's not going to be any more bodies, it all ends here."

"And we are not going to pursue it any further," Jones said.

"We're not?" Recker asked.

"No. We're not. I know what's going on in that head of yours."

"Oh yeah?"

"Yes. You're thinking Vincent is behind it and you're thinking about confronting him about it."

"And I shouldn't do that?"

"No. Why put the relationship you've built up with him in jeopardy over something we don't know whether we should even be involved in to begin with? Let's move on."

"What do you think actually happened?" Haley asked.

"I think Vincent found someone he could pin this whole mess on. Then he made sure it somehow got back to me about Flowers, which is why Tyrell got the info so cheap. Then I'm thinking he sent his right-hand man over there to finish the job, plant some evidence, tie it off."

"Malloy."

"Yeah. Now, everyone sleeps easier, his competition's eliminated, nobody suspects him, like I said... all neat and tidy."

"Like David said, there's nothing else we can really do at this point."

"I know. Doesn't mean I have to like it, though."

Recker's phone then rang.

"What can I help you with, Detective?"

"Just wanted to say thanks for helping out with this," Andrews answered. "Don't know if we would've gotten to this point without you."

"Just glad I could help."

"Well, a lot of the boys down here wish they could thank you."

"Not sure I really deserve any thanks," Recker said.

"I know I said I hoped to have him alive and take him in, but there's quite a few of us who wanted to do what you did, anyway."

"What makes you think it was me?"

"Who else would it have been?" Andrews asked. "I know you like to play it coy and all and can't admit to anything. But just to let you know, I think you've got a few extra converts to your fan club down here."

"Always nice to know."

"Anyway, just wanted to say thanks. I don't suppose we'll continue to get a chance to work on any things together?"

"Not likely," Recker said. "You can probably toss that phone now. It'll go off the grid in a few days."

"Well, good luck to you. If you ever wind up at my desk, I'll conveniently forget to lock your cuffs or something."

Recker laughed. "I appreciate that."

After hanging up, Recker, though disappointed with the conclusion of the case, seemed to be ready to move on.

"I guess it's on to bigger and better things?"

"Yes," Jones answered. "I have several things going on now. Should have another case to work on by tomorrow."

"Great."

"The detective say anything interesting?"

"Ah, usual. Everyone thinks it was me that did it. Seems it's bought me a few extra friends on the force should I ever need them."

"Well, I guess that is a perk should it ever be needed."

"Yeah. Seems as though everyone thinks I'm a hero. Even when I'm not."

ABOUT THE AUTHOR

Mike Ryan lives in Pennsylvania with his wife, four kids, and three dogs. He is always working on his next novel. Visit his website at www.mikeryanbooks.com to find out more about his books, and sign up for his newsletter.

facebook.com/mikeryanauthor

instagram.com/mikeryanauthor

ALSO BY MIKE RYAN

The Cain Series

The Eliminator Series

The Ghost Series

The Extractor Series

The Brandon Hall Series

The Cari Porter Series

The Last Job

A Dangerous Man

The Crew

Printed in Great Britain
by Amazon

22403553R00145